THE HADFIELD SERIES

First Edition April 2021

Developmental Edit by Gray Plume Editing

Edited by Rare Bird Editing

Proofread by Magnolia Author Services

Cover design by The Swoonies Book Covers

Copyright © 2021 by Rachel Ann Smith

ISBN 978-1-951112-12-7

TEMPTING A GENTLEMAN

RACHEL ANN SMITH

PENFORD
PUBLISHING

CHAPTER ONE

*E*nsconced in the Hadfield drawing room, Emma sat stiffly on the edge of the ornate blue-velvet settee. The fine furniture was a far cry from the well-worn wooden bench she and her best friend Bronwyn, now Countess Hadfield, used to occupy for afternoon tea. She'd rather be huddled about the kitchen table at the back of Bronwyn's parents' shop than be worried about messin' up the plush fabric that cushioned her bottom.

Emma stared over Bronwyn's shoulder at a portrait upon the wall. She guessed it was a close male relation to the current Lord Hadfield as they shared a similar rakish smile. Emma hadn't yet met Bronwyn's brother-in-law, Christopher Neale, although she'd heard plenty about him. Bronwyn yammered on. "It's been six weeks, and not one of the countless overqualified candidates have passed Christopher's final interview."

Her friend since childhood, dressed in one of Emma's

latest satin creations, paced about the luxurious room. It was easily three times the size of Emma's parents' parlor, and while Bronwyn looked at ease in her new home, Emma would prefer to be back on the east end of town. Bronwyn paraded back and forth in front of the stern paintings of past Hadfield family members, her forthright march tamed to a ladylike walk. Her friend had undergone other subtle changes since marrying the head of the Protectors of the Royal Family—PORFs—but Bronwyn had vowed she remained the same and would remain Emma's best friend until her last breath. Bound by an oath taken years ago, Emma was compelled to support Bronwyn in any and every way possible. But even if she hadn't sworn to serve and protect PORFs, Emma would not abandon her best friend. Even if it meant she had to endure the back-aching pain of being perched on the edge of a formal settee for over an hour listening to Bronwyn's complaints. Emma held in her sigh.

Bronwyn swiveled to face her. "I swear my brother-in-law is purposefully scaring each and every applicant away."

She wanted to cross her arms and glare at Bronwyn, but that would not be ladylike nor becoming. Instead, she calmly crossed her ankles and said, "Ye only have yerself to blame. Ye was too good of a legal secretary, working all hours without complaint."

Bronwyn's eyes narrowed—Emma had obviously failed to mask her irritation. The clean, freshly redecorated Hadfield drawing room walls were closing in. It had been two decades since she had stepped foot into a townhouse on the west end. The knots in Emma's shoulders tightened. She had been but a toddler of three or four, holding her mum's hand tightly while being escorted into the Hereford library. The wife of the man who sired Emma had learned of her existence and summoned them in the middle of the night. It wasn't until years later that Emma understood the old biddy's threats and demands.

Exhaling slowly, Emma refocused on the blur of green silk as Bronwyn continued to flounce about the room. She hadn't shared that night's events with another soul, even her closest friend. No one would understand the anger and shame that night had evoked. And she'd be damned if she'd let anyone make her feel that way ever again. But she wasn't in the Hereford townhouse. She was safe in the company of her dearest friend, who had managed to infuse warmth into the cold, aristocratic room. Wall panels covered in paper etched with an intricate pattern that reminded Emma of wild daisies. Thick, royal-blue window coverings with complementary cream and aquamarine for the delicate upholstery. But it all spoke of wealth and Bronwyn's new station within the ton.

Emma shifted, planting her foot firmly on the Persian rug to prevent her knee from bobbing up and down. If she didn't love Bronwyn like a sister, she wouldn't even *consider* enduring hours upon hours of torture, let alone subject herself to the misery. Until today, Bronwyn had accommodated Emma's wish to conduct their visits on the east end of town. When Emma received the missive early this morn conveying Bronwyn's invitation for tea, she couldn't delay the inevitable.

All rules regarding etiquette thrown out the window, Bronwyn stomped over to Emma and glared down at her. "You meant that as a compliment, I'm sure."

"Luv a dove. Just tell Mr. Neale to settle." Emma's lips curved into a smirk. It was good to see her old friend's fiery nature again.

Bronwyn removed one hand from her hip and waved it about in a circle. "Everyone thinks Christopher is the easygoing brother and my husband the demanding one when, in fact, it is the other way around." Bronwyn flopped into the wing-backed chair facing Emma and flung her arms wide. With the return of her old ways, the woman cared not that her skirts were askew and her cap sleeve had slipped precariously to the edge of the PORF mark. Bronwyn had purposefully chosen her upper arm, the least discreet of places upon her body, as a challenge to Emma. A challenge she had welcomed.

Emma snorted. "Ye're in love. Blinded to yer bloomin' husband's faults."

Unable to relax despite the return of their childhood familiarity, Emma extended her leg and then curled one ankle behind the other. "At least Lord Hadfield demanded he receive the PORF mark and gain the responsibilities along with it as soon as he was made aware of them, unlike his brother." The need to remain on guard steeled her spine and added an unnecessary edge to her tone.

Bronwyn raised her brows. "You know Landon

would prefer you address him by his first name. *And* you are aware that my husband won't hear of Christopher receiving the mark until he is wed. And in typical Neale fashion, my brother-in-law will only marry for love."

Bah. The Head PORF, no matter his relation to Bronwyn, would always command her respect. And what was Bronwyn babbling on about? Marriage. Love. None of that mattered. The man had a duty. Christopher was next in line to inherit the Hadfield title and PORF responsibilities until Bronwyn birthed a son. It was well known that the Neale men never lived long. If she were in Christopher's position, she would demand the right to fulfill a generations-old oath to protect the royal family. Instead, the man abided by his brother's wishes with no objection. It left Emma with no desire to meet Bronwyn's brother-in-law, despite her friend's efforts to contrive an introduction between them.

"How do ye suppose Mr. Neale will find a wife if he can't bloomin' well find a secretary?"

"That is a valid point." Bronwyn's facial muscles twitched and contorted until Emma was pierced with one of Bronwyn's I-have-a-plan looks. "Aha! If Christopher weren't plagued by both searches, his temperament would be much improved. I shall redirect my efforts to finding him a wife. Once he is wed, he'll be more amicable."

"Are you implying that Mr. Neale is in need of..." Emma wagged her eyebrows.

"I am. I am indeed. Men are much more accommodating if they are...well... Never mind. You are an innocent. I shouldn't be speaking of such things."

Bronwyn's words poked at a bruise upon Emma's heart. They no longer shared a similar position within the Network. They lived on opposite sides of London. And while Bronwyn had never shown an interest in beaus or marriage, she was the first to find love and a partner in life. The ache in her chest spurred Emma's retort. "Oh my, ain't ye all hoity-toity now. Yer lady rules don't apply when ye are speakin' with me. *And* according to *my* Network sources, Mr. Neale is well acquainted with a number of widows. He has been spied visiting Madam Sinclair's establishment on occasion. I doubt a wife will make a difference."

"I can assure you, Christopher is well beyond his wild days, and since Landon left the law firm to him to run, Christopher's only mistress has been work. In fact, his work ethic reminds me of someone I know rather well." Bronwyn arched an eyebrow.

Bronwyn's defense of her new brother-in-law didn't surprise Emma, but to believe the Network's information on the man was utterly wrong was highly unusual.

"Speakin' of work, I'd best be gettin' back to the shop." Emma rose. Blood rushed to her legs, causing sharp prickling sensations along the backs of her knees. "Please don't bother calling for a coach to be readied. It'll be quicker if I simply take a hackney."

Bronwyn stood and reached for her hands. "I've one more favor to ask before you leave." Serious blue eyes bored into Emma. "I can't postpone it any longer; I must host a ball, and I want you to attend."

Good Heavens—*a ball*. The blood drained from her hands, leaving them cold and clammy in her friend's grasp. "Ye know I'd lay me life down for ye, but I'll not attend a ball amongst me clients."

She could hardly manage being here when it was just the two of them. Surrounded by socialites, she'd find the walls of Hadfield townhouse even more restricting. To stand amongst those for whom she acted as modiste? She wanted nothing to do with their world. It was a world of ruthlessness, deceit, and greed. It was the reason why PORFs and the Network established themselves apart as separate organizations many generations ago. No. She couldn't do it. Emma shook her head. "Not even if ye ordered me to. I'd rather face the Network elders' council and risk banishment than parade meself before the eyes of the ton."

Bronwyn's shoulders sagged as she released Emma's hands. "I understand."

Blimey. The simple, undemanding statement stole all of Emma's bluster and replaced it with guilt for denying her friend her support. Placing her hands behind her, Emma clasped them tightly and inhaled deeply to fortify her nerves. "I don't know how to dance."

Bronwyn's watery blue eyes lit up. Her friend blinked, and Emma's lips curved into a smile. Years of kinship returned. Emma found herself engulfed in a hug similar to the one Bronwyn had bestowed upon her a year ago when Bronwyn turned one-and-twenty, and Emma had gifted Bronwyn with a box of chocolates. The woman's secret weakness.

The latch of the door squeaked, and Emma pulled away.

Bouncing on her toes, Bronwyn exclaimed, "I'll hire us a dance master."

Lord Hadfield's warm voice came from the doorway. "Absolutely not. I'll not allow another man the pleasure. I shall teach you."

"Very well, we'll hire one for Emma then."

Bronwyn's husband entered and came to stand next to his wife. Without hesitation, Bronwyn rose onto her tiptoes and greeted Lord Hadfield with a kiss square on the lips.

The man's cheeks reddened as he smiled lovingly down at his wife. "I think I know the perfect candidate. I shall make the arrangements."

Emma took two steps back, hoping to sneak out of the room. She froze when Lord Hadfield turned and addressed her. "Emma. It's a pleasure to see you again."

Blushing at the display of overt love and care, she tried not to stare at the man's charming dimple but failed. Remembering her manners, Emma bent at the knees in what she hoped was a graceful curtsy. "Lord Hadfield, ye've no need to hire a..."

He raised a hand, halting the rest of her protest. "I know I've already asked, but I'll *ask* again. Please refer to me by my given name."

Emma bobbed her head. "Ye don't need to waste yer coin on me."

"If it makes my wife happy, I'll gladly pay a fortune for dance lessons, but as it happens, this dance master owes me a favor, and he is extremely reliable and discreet." He wrapped an arm around Bronwyn's waist as he spoke. Lord Hadfield didn't even attempt to hide his love and affection for his wife. No. It was blatantly clear he was infatuated with Bronwyn.

Her best friend was known for being intensely private and guarded even among the Network. Yet Bronwyn stood at ease next to Lord Hadfield. Emma had never had to share Bronwyn's regard with anyone before. Emma glanced about the room once more. Lord Hadfield was Bronwyn's new family and world.

She didn't fit in here. Emma blinked away the threat of tears. She needed to leave before Bronwyn detected her upset. Emma grabbed her shawl that lay over the arm of the settee and said, "That is very generous of you both, but with the season in full swing, I'm rather busy."

As Emma wrapped the material about her shoulders, she caught sight of tears welling in Bronwyn's eyes. Damn the woman. From the beginning of their friendship, they'd been highly in tune with each other's feelings as if they connected intangibly. If one felt hurt or happy, so did the other. Blast. If the roles had been reversed, Bronwyn would do anything for Emma.

Emma put her pride aside. "Gah. Stop yer waterworks. I'll make time for yer bloomin' dance master." Crisscrossing the material in front of her, she asked, "How long is it til yer blasted ball?"

Lord Hadfield answered, "Three weeks from today. I

believe I can even arrange for the instructor to give you lessons at your shop. After hours, of course. If that would suit you."

"Hmph. I guess I can move things about to make room at the shop."

"Splendid." Bronwyn clapped her hands with glee. "I'll be by tomorrow for my fitting."

"Ye'll have to pay extra if ye want a new gown completed in three weeks."

Lord Hadfield beamed down at his wife. "I'll happily pay extra." Displaying his irresistible dimple, he asked, "Shall I have the instructor come by tomorrow eve?"

It was no wonder the man had been a successful barrister before he had inherited an earldom and assumed the role of Head PORF. Oath or no oath, no one in their right mind would deny the man standing before her.

Emma answered, "Aye."

Before the PORF couple could issue any other asinine orders, she turned, marched out of the room, and fled.

CHAPTER TWO

*T*he coach ride from Neale & Sons to the Hadfield townhouse was one Christopher Neale had taken many a time over the last two years since his brother Landon inherited the earldom. Today, the trip took twice as long as it should. Overcrowded carriages jostled for space and pedestrians milled about as if they hadn't a care in the world. It was not long ago he too led an untroubled life. However, recently it seemed he was constantly being summoned or ordered about, no longer the master of his own life.

Melancholy and disbelief over his cousin Baldwin's death lingered despite the changes to both his and Landon's lives. He wasn't supposed to be the one in charge of running the firm. That had been Landon's destiny, not his. He had basked and excelled at leading the life of a second son. Yes, he had attended Oxford and attended the obligatory classes to obtain his law degree, a family tradition. Still, his passions had always lain in the arts and trade negotiations. He had happily managed civil suits while leaving case law and court appearances to Landon. But the day their uncle passed, Landon had inherited not only a bankrupt estate but also a generations-old duty to protect the royal family. A familial duty neither of them were informed of until their cousin Theo was about to forgo love for duty. Even before assuming the role of Head PORF, Landon had demanded Christopher wed before receiving the mark of a PORF, claiming it was in his best interest. While it irked him, Christopher admired and respected Landon, and so he agreed to delay receiving the mark until he found a suitable wife. For men of the Neale linage, that meant a lady he would love until his last breath. But after two years of searching and one failed courtship, Christopher was no longer willing to wait.

The coach slowed at the driver's command, "Whoa!"

Before the coach came to a complete stop, Christopher jumped out, ready to extract the information his mama had sent him to obtain.

He placed a booted foot on the first step, and the wide door of the townhouse flung open, revealing the petite form of a cloaked woman. Her hood fluttered, concealing her features as she scanned the street and the path before her. Before Christopher's foot landed upon the second step, the woman fled down the stairs and past him in such a frenzied blur he hadn't managed to ascertain her identity.

The hairs on his arms stood on end, and his heart fluttered as if an electric current had run through him. The jolt froze him in place as the woman's vehicle disappeared down the road. With a shake of his head, Christopher turned and mounted the steps to the front door. On the landing, he glanced back down the road. The bizarre thought that he had let something—no, some*one*—important slip away had him stomping through the foyer. Preoccupied with sorting his rioting thoughts, Christopher handed over his coat and hat to the butler and meandered towards the family drawing room. The floral scent lingered in the air, tickling his nose. His body tingled as if he was experiencing an aftershock. How was that possible? He hadn't caught a clear glimpse of her features, yet every cell from head to toe seemed to come alive as she breezed by him. No one of his acquaintance in all his nine and twenty years on this earth had ever evoked this strange physical reaction within him.

With his hand poised on the door latch, Bronwyn's gleeful laughter filtered through the wood door. He swung the drawing room door open, only to find his sister-in-law tangled up in his brother's arms yet again. Even after six weeks of marital bliss, the couple was still intolerable.

Clearing his throat, Christopher said, "Pray tell me the name of the young lady that nearly barreled me over in her haste to leave your residence?"

Bronwyn said, "Oh, that would have been Emma. Did you introduce yourself?"

"Hardly. She ran right past me as if the devil was on her heels and launched herself into a hack that was out front...." Christopher frowned. "A hack, not your coach."

Landon chuckled. "Emma refuses to the use of our coach, so I purchased a vehicle that resembled a hack. Not to worry, she will be safely delivered home."

There was a lot of information to be gleaned from his brother's reply. However, it didn't explain the extraordinary burst of energy he experienced as the woman passed him. Christopher wasn't versed in the paranormal, but having a friend who could see and speak to the dead broadened one's mind. Perhaps he was overthinking the woman's effect upon him. No, the sparks of interest the mystery woman evoked within him were the first feelings he'd experienced other than ennui since Lady Arabelle's rejection over six months ago.

Lady Arabelle—the lady he had hoped would be the solution to his marriage dilemma. She was musically inclined and they shared many of the same interests. For a short period, he'd managed to convince himself he was in love with the woman. Even persuaded himself to offer for her hand, only to find out she had given her heart to another.

Bronwyn's smile faltered as her gaze settled upon him. "Why have you come to visit?" His sister-in-law's voice was filled with worry.

"Mama sent me over to find out why the two of you missed church this morn." He refrained from admitting he'd stopped by the offices along the way, intending to see to a few minor matters, only to have stayed for most of the day. He really did need to hire a new legal secretary.

"Bronwyn wasn't feeling well." Landon smiled,

revealing the irritating dimple that meant his wife was hale, and there was naught to worry about.

"More likely the two of you simply didn't care to leave your bed. You'll have to plead your own forgiveness from Mama then." Unable to banish his curiosity, Christopher asked, "Why was your friend leaving in such haste?"

Bronwyn's eyes lit up, love for her friend clear as day. "Landon has ordered her to attend dance lessons. She's agreed to attend my very first ball."

Landon's hand fell upon Christopher's shoulder. "Emma requires an instructor who I can trust to be discreet."

"You can't be serious. I've got a full case workload, and without the assistance of a full-time assistant, I'm buried in research."

"Emma will be a quick learner. An hour or two twice a week should suffice. She is expecting you to arrive after her shop closes tomorrow eve."

His brother was fully aware he'd not deny any request. "Why are you asking this of me?"

Landon ticked the reasons off on three fingers:. "Because you are an adept dancer. You need the exercise. And I know of no one else whose charm can set Emma at ease. We are asking her to be subjected to a night with the piranhas, and I want the woman to be prepared."

All reasonable and valid arguments but superfluous. His sister-in-law's pleading eyes were asking, not demanding. From the day Bronwyn entered Neale & Sons and insisted on the opportunity to apply for the position of legal secretary, Christopher knew she'd become family one day. Except it took his damn brother eight years to come to his senses and offer for her. It was a prime example of how their lives worked. Matters simply fell into place for Landon, while Christopher's existence was a game of chess, requiring him to continually readjust his strategy to achieve his goal: a life beyond the shadows of his big brother and the traditions of the Neale family.

Christopher narrowed his gaze upon his sister-in-law, who had uncharacteristically remained quiet. "Please tell me this is not a matchmaking scheme."

Squaring her shoulders, Bronwyn donned a look of seriousness, but the sparkle in her eyes was pure mischief. "Emma is extremely wary of outsiders. She trusts no one but those who have been fully investigated by the Network. We need your help."

Landon grinned again, revealing his darn dimple. "Love, a wonderful retort." He asked Christopher, "Will you be joining us for supper?"

Ignoring his brother, Christopher rephrased his concern. "Dear sister, do you deny this is an attempt to see me happily wed?"

"Not everything is about you, dear brother. This is about Emma and my wish for her."

Bronwyn had obviously been honing her skill at the art of word manipulation, having married Landon. Christopher couldn't deny that Landon and Bronwyn standing together were a formidable force. The intimate looks and subtle nonverbal cues between the couple were a reminder of the type of relationship Christopher should be seeking. He had been a fool to think a union with Lady Arabelle would have sufficed. A wavy, pinkish blur appeared around the pair as if they were radiating some type of shield. Emma's cloaked form came to mind. He'd not experienced a jolt of energy from another as acute as when Emma had passed him by out front. It was as if his body was tuned, like a pianoforte, to hers. If he danced with Emma, would they glow like his brother and sister-in-law? There was only one way to find out—he'd have to play dance master.

The arch of Landon's brow brought Christopher's thoughts in line. If he were to acquiesce to his brother's request, he might as well bargain for his sister-in-law's time. "Very well, I shall provide dance lessons, but in return, I'll need Bronwyn's assistance in the office. Not merely to search for her replacement but to actually perform case summaries."

Bronwyn's lips curved into a smug smile as if she had anticipated his demand for her help.

Landon nodded and turned to his wife. "So long as you work reasonable hours and promise not to overdo."

"I promise. But you might want to clarify for Christopher what you deem reasonable—for I believe his sense of time is skewed."

"No earlier than nine and no later than four in the afternoon."

"That is but half a day." Christopher let the words slip before he caught sight of Landon's scowl. "You used to have her working from the crack of dawn until well past the supper hour."

"My wife needs her rest. And need I remind you that if she is at the offices too late in the day, it will mean you will have to contend also with Mama and Theo. For they shall want to consult with Bronwyn on the details for the ball."

"I don't need them meddling in my affairs. Nine to three shall do." With Bronwyn's help, perhaps he might gain an hour or two of sleep.

Linking her arm into the crook of Christopher's, Bronwyn ushered him to stroll about the room. "Emma's last fittings are scheduled for four, which means her clients should be gone by seven-thirty, eight at the latest. You will want to leave the office early to make the jaunt across town."

All hopes of extra rest were dashed. Dance lessons plus travel time would negate the hours gained from Bronwyn's assistance. His only solace was Landon's assessment that Emma was a quick study. Perhaps she would only require an evening or two of instruction.

Bronwyn stopped and squeezed his arm. "You are working too much and not eating enough. Please stay for supper."

"Emma's day ends rather late. What time does it begin?" What an asinine question. Why did he care?

She released her hold on him. "Five in the morn." Bronwyn padded back to the settee, where she gracefully sank to sit next to Landon, who observed with interest. "She's not normally abed until ten in the eve, so if you arrive at eight, there should be little disruption to her schedule."

"Glad we are all worried about Emma's commitments."

"She is my dearest friend. No. Emma is like a sister to me. I only want the best for her."

Bronwyn's choice of words was rather peculiar. Christopher linked his hands together behind his back. "And that is why you insisted she attend *your* debut ball."

"You think me selfish," Bronwyn countered. She rose and mimicked his posture, her hands clasped behind her back. Preparing to debate like they used to in order to ready Christopher for a case at court.

"I don't wish to argue, sister." He caught sight of the light shadows beneath her eyes. "Are you well? You look rather...tired." He faced Landon, "Did you call the doctor?" Landon didn't appear remotely concerned.

"Aye. He said Bronwyn will be right as rain in another nine months, maybe ten."

"Huzzah. I'm to be an uncle." Christopher beamed. He'd always wanted to be an uncle. Unlike his brother, he wanted children. It was the wife that Christopher was wary about.

Although Lady Arabelle Risley had granted him a kiss or two and claimed his working station did not matter to her, she had made it clear that she wasn't interested in marriage—at least not to him. The woman had a terrible crush on the renowned rake Lord Markin-son. It had been Christopher's suggestion to make Markinson jealous with well-timed kisses. While the kisses hadn't been heart pounding nor soul shattering, he'd still been disappointed when Arabelle rejected any talk of his suit. But if his sources were correct, Markinson planned to reform and court Arabelle properly. He loved being right and when a plan worked, but in this instance, it only served as a reminder that being in the right was rather lonely. Watching his brother's and sister-in-law's fawning smiles as they shared the news of the babe reinforced the emptiness that he sought to fill.

Bronwyn leaned up against Landon as she addressed Christopher. "I'm in the early stages yet, and we had not intended to share the news until I'm a little further along. This will not impact my commitment to assist you. It is vital Emma learn how to dance, and...perhaps you could assist her in refining her speech as you did with me?"

Yes, Emma had been wise to run. If he stayed any longer, he dreaded to consider what other tasks would be assigned to him.

"I'll see what I can do." He pulled out his pocket watch and checked the time. "I need to be off; otherwise, I shall be late."

Landon and Bronwyn simultaneously rose, but it was Landon who spoke. "Where are you off to? Join us for supper."

"Sorry; I can't. I'm to meet Lord Thornton at Brooks's. He's yet again managed to render his wife enceinte, which will make for child number five, and the man insists on having his will redrafted with every addition to the family. Which reminds me—we will have to have your papers redrawn up. Bronwyn, will you add it to the list of tasks for tomorrow?"

His sister-in-law nodded with a side glance to her husband.

Landon flashed his dastardly dimple and said, "Perhaps I'll draft the revisions myself. No need to add to your load, little brother."

"Do you remember how to handle such menial tasks, old man?" Christopher pinned Landon with a sardonic glare.

He loved sparring with Landon. They hadn't had much chance lately. Not with Landon having to deal with more important issues like running an ever-increasing estate, and of course, oversight of the PORFs.

Landon bristled. "I'm not that old."

Bronwyn gave a slight shake of her head and smiled up at her husband. "Let's not delay Christopher any longer, my love."

The intervention soothed his brother's wounded feelings. After a curt bow, Christopher bid the couple good day and turned to make a hasty departure.

Landon, of course, had to have the last word. "Don't forget about Emma."

Christopher closed the door behind him. He had nothing but admiration for his big brother in how he handled matters, but to demand Christopher play dance master was really pushing the bounds of familial duty.

Accepting Morris's help in donning his great coat, Christopher stood and pondered his predicament. Releasing a sigh, Christopher admitted Landon's ask paled in comparison to the enormous task of dealing with an absent PORF. The unusual decision by the current Lord Burke to move abroad placed significantly more pressure upon the remaining two PORF families. Christopher wanted to assist Landon. But his stubborn brother had not yet granted his approval for Christopher to receive the mark of a PORF. Landon remained steadfast in his declaration: in order for Christopher to become an official PORF, he must wed. Which meant he'd have to redouble his efforts to figure out how one went about searching for love.

CHAPTER THREE

*E*mma ran her thumb over the ridges of the stamped symbol of the Network—a harped angel set into the silver button. A heavy sigh escaped her as she attached the button reserved for dresses to be worn by PORFs. Lifting up Bronwyn's new ball gown by the puff sleeves, Emma inspected her work. Both seams and buttons were carefully hidden. But to her eye, the design lacked a certain flair that she'd previously managed to infuse in all of Bronwyn's creations. Emma's creativity relied heavily on her mood and her knowledge of the client. Bronwyn had changed, and so had Emma's designs for the woman. She was a pea goose to have believed that nothing would change between them. She and Bronwyn had been a dynamic pair within the Network, but now Bronwyn was Lord Hadfield's partner and a PORF.

The prospect of one day sitting on the Elder Council no longer held any appeal. In fact, most days, little to nothing held Emma's interest. Even negotiating and bartering with Mr. Hains, the cloth merchant, her favorite monthly event, proved unsatisfying. Her business was booming, with word spreading amongst the ton of her personalized designs as opposed to dresses fashioned from boring old fashion plates. Despite her success, which required her to work long, exhausting hours, Emma's priority remained first and foremost to the Network, providing disguises and uniforms worn by its members. What was her purpose—to serve PORFs and one day be a Network elder or to design and create stunning creations for the ladies of the ton? Or neither, for they both had lost their appeal.

The grandfather clock in the corner showed nearly eight o'clock. She folded the ball gown and placed it carefully in a box to be delivered to the Hadfield townhouse. Her shoulders sagged as she scanned the shoproom floor that she had worked hard to clear for the evening dance lessons. All her efforts were for naught. Billy had arrived earlier in the afternoon with bolts and bolts of material she had successfully negotiated to purchase from Mr. Hains. With no time to rearrange, the dance lessons would have to take place in the small parlor above stairs, next to her private living quarters. Emma questioned the wisdom in inviting a stranger, and a man at that, into her sanctuary. But she trusted Bronwyn and her husband to have chosen a dance master who wouldn't take advantage of the situation. She'd made inquiries, but the Network rumor mill was peculiarly lacking in knowledge as to whom Lord Hadfield had employed to teach her how to dance.

Like clockwork at a quarter to eight, her dad walked into the shop. "Hallo, Em. Ye alone already?" He came over and gave her a big bear hug. Her dad was a barrel-chested man with a body that resembled a man of thirty, not of his six and fifty years.

As Emma pulled back, her dad attempted to peer up into the loft. Her mother never spoke of the man who sired her, and Emma never cared to bring up the topic. She considered Mr. Benjamin Lennox her dad, and the man loved Emma as if she were his own. Overprotective and loving, even after her years of solitary living, Emma's dad still didn't care for her decision to live alone at the shop.

"Aye. I kicked the lovely Lady Arabelle out an hour ago." She stepped around his bulky form and retrieved a parcel wrapped in brown cloth. "I heard Brian and Baxter have outgrown their trousers." She handed over the clothing for her siblings and slipped him a small satchel filled with coin. "I'm sorry, it's a little less this week. Bronwyn has ordered me to attend her first ball, and I had to purchase material for me gown."

"It's about time ye spent a little on yerself." He gave her back the pouch. "We can do without this week; go spend it on shoes or the like."

Emma glanced at the clock once more. She needed to be rid of her dad before the dance master arrived. Shoving the money back into her dad's hands, she said, "If I'm in need of such flipantry, I'll just take it out of next week's amount. Now get home before Mum's dinner gets cold."

"Aye, yer mum will be piping mad if I'm late. Are ye sure about the blunt?"

"Yes. Now git." She pushed her dad out the door, and he hovered until she swung the sign in the door to closed, and the three latches clicked into place.

Her dad worked odd jobs for the Network, and her mum was busy raising six growing children, four of them boys. Without her assistance, her family would have to rely heavily on the Network. Her mum was the proud descendant of a founding member—Emma would rather starve than to seek out help. No. She wouldn't let her family accept charity, even though her mum preached that wealth comes in a multitude of forms and the Network recognizes that. Not was not the case in the upper classes—Coin was king. And when the coffers of the wealthy dwindled, they married to replenish them.

Drawing the curtains closed, she saw the shadow of a rather tall gentleman approaching. For some odd reason, she had expected the dance master to be slim and of average height. Pressing her back to the door, she waited.

Three quick raps followed by a pause and then one solid knock. It was indeed the dance master. Quickly releasing the locks, she swung open the door. What the blazes! Mr. Christopher Neale, brother to the bloomin' Head PORF, stood on her doorstep. Oh, she recognized the man; he was cut from the same cloth as his brother. The corner of Mr. Neale's lips curled into a charming grin, and Emma would be a liar if she didn't admit to the spark of interest that fluttered in her chest. Brow furrowed, she poked her head out and scanned the area.

Mr. Neale twisted and looked about the stoop, removing his hat and gloves. "Are you going to invite me in?"

Up close, Emma noted Mr. Neale's warm brown eyes, fine aristocratic nose, and his firm but inviting full lips—he was a handsome devil all right, as reported amongst the Network members. Women were rumored to swoon in his presence, and now she understood why. Attempting to gather her wits, she moved behind the door as Mr. Neale barged in.

Emma sputtered, "What the devil are ye doing here? Lord Hadfield advised I was to expect a dance master, not a gentleman known for dallyin' about."

He simply smiled and proceeded further into the shop. Mr. Neale didn't possess a charming dimple like his brother, but the curve of his lips had a profound effect upon her pulse.

"So you already know who I am. Shall we skip the formalities? You may call me Christopher, and I shall address you by your given name. Emma, correct?"

Her ire burst into flames—the audacity of the man to look and speak to her as if she were a pea goose. Except the twinkle in the man's eyes blanketed her flash of anger, bringing her rage to a mere simmer. She agreed with a curt nod.

With a lopsided smile, he said, "I assure you I'm quite proficient at dancing and an adept teacher. Landon, in his infinite wisdom, believed discretion would be best in this situation. We wouldn't want anyone outside of our circle to know, now would we?"

The man was a barrister. Perhaps if she used some of the knowledge she'd learned from Bronwyn, it might help place them on more equal footing. Because that damned smile was turning her insides to mush.

Facing the closed door and taking her time to turn each lock, Emma asked, "If I feign a momentary lapse in sanity, do ye believe I'd be able to avoid attendin' Bronwyn's ball?"

When she turned back around, his gaze was trained entirely upon her—assessing. Her cheeks burned under his scrutiny.

Tapping his hat against his leg, Mr. Neale answered, "In this case, such a plea will do you no good."

The spark of energy she had been lacking reappeared. "Then wot would ye advise?" Something about Mr. Neale provoked her to want to spar with him, both verbally and physically. He would be a fine opponent.

The flare of interest in his eyes was unmistakable. She hadn't meant to evoke such a response. Emma took in a shallow breath to quiet her nerves that had sparked to life and on alert. He was an honorable gentleman. He was a rake. Being the product of a gentleman's seduction, she would not fall for the gentleman's charms.

Bustling past him, she twirled about. It wouldn't be safe to bring him above stairs. Safe for whom—her or him? She would have to figure out an alternative.

Mr. Neale removed his greatcoat and folded it over the waiting room settee. Emma couldn't help but stare at his handsome, lithe form as he strode over to stand by the measuring table. "There's not much room in here." His gaze roamed the room and then narrowed upon her. "Is something the matter?"

"I had a hectic day, and I've not had a chance to rearrange things for the lesson."

Mr. Neale looked about once more and removed his jacket. The man would be naked before the hour was up if he continued to remove articles of clothing. She imagined he'd be a fine specimen to look upon with those shoulders and narrow waist. She snapped her wayward thoughts back to the matter at hand. She was being ridiculous.

Chuckling, he asked, "Care to share your thoughts?"

His warm, teasing tone sent blood rushing to her cheeks. Emma shook her head in response.

He prowled about the room and then stopped at the foot of the stairs that led up to her private chambers. "Do you sleep here?"

Voice lost to the pounding of her heart, Emma nodded.

"All alone?" Mr. Neale's relaxed demeanor fled, replaced by a deep frown. "With no one about who would protect you from thieves?"

"I can protect meself."

"Humph." He placed a foot on the first step.

"Wait. Where do ye fink yer going?"

"To search for an appropriate space for us to practice, of course."

"But..."

He didn't wait. He marched up the stairs and called down, "Come along, Emma. You have the perfect area up here. We don't have much time, and since this is extremely important to Bronwyn and, in turn, my brother and thus to me...we shall need every minute you can spare."

Damnation. Were all the men in the Neale family overbearing? She trudged up the stairs and found Mr. Neale dressed merely in his lawn shirt and trousers. His waistcoat and cravat draped over the back of the solitary wooden chair tucked neatly under her small writing desk. He dominated the small space with his size, yet he waltzed about the room as if he belonged in her private retreat. Inexplicably, Emma remained frozen on the top step. His lithe form mesmerized and thrilled her. He exuded confidence that he was probably born with. When she found herself the recipient of a charming smile that smashed her defenses, she stepped forward to the center of the loft and waited. Her heartbeat raced as he stepped forward and reached out for her hand. Ashamed of her rough hands from hours of sewing, she pulled them out of his reach and crisscrossed them at the small of her back.

Christopher asked, "Tell me, have you any experience at all?" His lips curved back into an irresistible grin. Memories flooded her mind, of boys' lips pressed against hers as they attempted what they called kisses. No experience kissing a man like Mr. Neale.

"Emma? Have you any experience dancing before?"

"Nay. I'm afraid I've none. Ye'll have to start with the very basics."

He circled her.

Face-to-face again, he tilted his head to the side. "May I have this dance, Emma?"

She stared at his hand—palm up. His fingers were long and uncallused. She'd never cared before that her hands were not silky smooth. She whirled about to retrieve the elbow-length gloves that lay upon her tidy desk.

Tugging them on as if she was donning armor, she smiled and placed her gloved hand in his.

The glimmer in his eyes dimmed. "Do you fear me?"

She shook her head.

His brow crinkled. "Are you sure?"

She shook her head without thought.

His chuckle relaxed her shoulders. "Bronwyn warned me you might be resistant to tutelage. I think we will get along just fine, but in order for our sessions to be successful, I'll need a little more communication from you. Part of achieving success at these god-awful ton events is executing the art of totally useless conversation. Remaining silent will relegate you to the outer walls with the wilting wallflowers. And you, my dear, are no wallflower."

"How do ye know I'm not?"

"Any friend of Bronwyn's must have nerves of steel. And you, Emma, are her dearest and closest friend, which means there is a clever mind in that pretty head of yours and a well-guarded heart." He pulled her closer and whispered, "I promise not to bite if you promise to smile."

Involuntarily her lips curved, and the man she had believed to be Lord Hadfield's puppet transformed into an enigmatic gentleman.

CHAPTER FOUR

*C*hristopher tried to tear his gaze from the woman's plump lips, which were made for devouring. He took in Emma's beautiful, tired features and was struck by the similarity of the woman's eye color to Arabelle's. Oddly, Emma also shared the honey-blonde hair that had lured him to endure countless ton affairs. But she wasn't Arabelle. Emma didn't hide her thoughts behind sweet, alluring smiles. No, the woman in his arms was like a Wordsworth poem, full of vitality with a strong undercurrent of passion. Emma was a refreshing change from the coy ladies he'd been subjected to over the past two years.

It was time to begin her lesson.

Christopher stepped back, placing a few inches between them. Space he needed to refocus his thoughts. Unable to release his hold on her hand, Christopher said, "The most fashionable couples' dance is the waltz.

However, there are two variations of the dance, the French and the German. With the limited time we have, it will be impossible to learn both, so we shall have to focus on the one most commonly danced, the French waltz."

"Why is it the most preferred?" Curious, intelligent eyes peered up at him. No simpering looks from Emma—no, she was direct and captivating.

Lost in her gaze, he absently answered, "The French version is slower in pace. It allows the gentleman ample opportunities to gaze into his partner's eyes."

Her brows creased in confusion. "Why would er man want to do *that*?"

"There is much you can say through one's gaze without words."

"Really? Such as?"

She was so innocent. He chuckled, which gained him a fierce frown from his partner.

"Your eyes tell me you are already irritated with me, and we haven't even begun dancing."

She tugged her hand out of his grasp. "Does the woman have to gaze back at the man?"

"Only if she wants to. In my experience, most ladies prefer to look into my eyes rather than at my cravat."

"Ye'd fink the ladies would get a crick in their neck."

He laughed. It was an astute observation, for, like Emma, most women only came up to the top of his shoulder. "There are four basic positions to the dance. Would you prefer I explain them or simply walk you through them?"

"Ye'd best explain first. Me brain and me feet are at odds most of the time."

He'd have to address her speech as Bronwyn had advised, but he quite enjoyed her almost lyrical accent. It made her rather unique. Instead of sounding harsh or coarse, Emma's cockney was a soft blend of vowels. He shook his head. He was here as a favor to his brother and sister-in-law, not for any other reason.

With nowhere to sit, he began to pace with his hands behind his back. "Right, the French waltz begins with a march of sorts. The starting position would have your right foot in front, heel turned towards me, while my left foot is in front with my heel turned towards you." He paused to demonstrate the awkward foot position. "Before we commence walking, I would place my right arm along the back part of your shoulder." With his arm stretched out, he continued, "Good gracious, this is silly. Come. Let us do this together."

Emma stiffly slid into place next to him, mirroring his pose. His body jerked. Emma's touch sent an intense bolt of vitality through to every nerve in his body. It wasn't a sensation of lust, but one akin to being shocked into motion. As if his body had been dormant, waiting solely for her. None of his reactions or thoughts made logical sense, but it was exhilarating, and he wanted to experience more. His body clearly desired to get closer to the woman, yet she remained distant and aloof. The thought of lowering her to the bare wooden floor and pleasuring her tempted him, but he was a gentleman, and she was Bronwyn's closest friend. He had never failed to lure a woman into granting him a kiss, yet he suspected his usual effortless charm and smile would garner him a solid left hook instead. Network women did not suffer fools, and he was here to dance, dammit, not kiss the woman.

But he needed a willing partner. Dancing required loose, fluid movements, and Emma's ramrod-straight back and stiff muscles would not do. Intuitively, he sensed he'd need to gain her trust first. The woman had remained wary ever since they went above stairs.

He turned to her. "I apologize. This is my first attempt at being a dance master, and I realize now I've come utterly unprepared. No music. No directions. Might I suggest we adjourn our lesson until tomorrow?"

She searched his features. "Did I do something wrong?"

"On the contrary, it is I who has gone about matters incorrectly."

Her eyes narrowed. "Seems to me ye're just bein' nice and ye've changed yer mind about teaching me. Ye're not the first gentleman to not want anythin' to do with me or to come near me." Shoulders straight, she whirled about and began descending the stairs.

Without time to ponder her words, he grabbed his garments and clattered down the stairs behind her.

The woman moved fast in skirts. She was waiting for him at the door. "I'll sort everythin' out with Bronwyn on the morrow."

He reached for his coat and slung it over the top of his arm along with his cravat and waistcoat. Grabbing his hat, he sauntered over to the door and stood next to her, closer than he should. His body once again reacted to her in perplexing ways.

"I'm uncertain what gave you the impression I've changed my mind, but I can assure you, there is no need to involve Bronwyn. I don't need her help. I'm quite capable of arranging for us to meet at an appropriate location that will allow us to properly conduct our lessons."

Emma raised her chin and said, "Mr. Neale, 'round these parts, we say wot we mean. No pretty words, just to the point. Ye understand?"

"I do." Instead of feelings of rejection, her fierce determination and bluntness made him want to get to know her better. She turned reached for the latch, but before she could open the door, he put his hand over hers. "I'm not ready to leave."

Her whole body shivered. The room temperature was pleasant, yet his blood ran hot with Emma mere inches away. Aghast at the idea she might fear him, he snatched his hand away. "Please allow me to stay, and we can discuss how we should move forward." As the words spilled out, Christopher questioned his own meaning.

Shoulders slumped forward. "I've got a full day tomorrow, so be quick and to the point." She glided past him and flopped into the wing back chair facing the dying fire.

He dropped his clothing on the settee, crouched by the embers, and blew. The flare of red told him the fire could be stoked back to life with a little encouragement. But could its mistress?

Once he had the fire roaring again, he turned back to see Emma intently staring into the flames.

She asked, "Do ye fink we could skip the lessons if I beg off sick the night of the ball?"

"You want me to lie to my brother?" He stood and commanded his feet to remain in place.

"No. Why would ye need to lie?"

"Because I'm expecting Landon to be waiting for me in my office at first light tomorrow. He'll be expecting a full report on our progress."

"Wotcha gonna tell him about this eve then?"

With a half-baked plan in mind, he replied, "The truth, of course. That we became acquainted, and that I intend to have directions with illustrations of the various positions sent over to you to study, and that we shall reconvene after work to practice."

"Where're ye getting these directions and pictures from?"

He puffed out his chest. "I'll be drafting them myself."

She let out a very unladylike guffaw. "Ye! I'm not sure stick figures will help me better understand yer long-winded explanations."

"Long-winded?"

"Aye. That's wot I said." She approached with a smirk that caught him off guard. Intrigued, he waited to see what she'd do next. Emma was beautiful when she let her guard down. She ran her hand along the outside of his arm. He slipped his hand into her small one and let her guide it to fall upon her waist. She looked straight into his eyes. "Ye didn't flinch. I don't bite either, but I heard ye might want to smile while ye dance."

He let her take the lead as she positioned his other hand on the other side of her delicate waist. He grinned and said, "I thought you said you had no experience."

"Is this how ye waltz?"

"Nay."

"I didn't fink so. But if yer not to be skittish about touchin' me, I thought this might set ye at ease."

Flinch? Skittish? Good lord, he wasn't a colt to be tamed. He was here to guide her. She was to be the student and he the master. How did matters get so turned about?

When she rested her gloved hands upon his upper arms, she fitted him perfectly. He swayed slightly, and she froze.

"To dance, we must move in unison. Follow my lead."

With the light pressure of his hands, he indicated which way she should move. Humming a melody, he pressed closer and led with his right leg forward, and within moments he found himself weaving her about the cramped room effortlessly. Never had he had a partner so in tune with his own body. Staring into her teal eyes, he spun her around for another two bars of the melody. His body vibrated in response to her closeness. Drawn by a magnetic pull, he lowered his head. Her lips were slightly parted, beckoning to him closer until their lips met. Her eyes closed at the soft pressure, and warmth blanketed his heart. For a split second, her features blurred with those of Arabelle's, and he stumbled.

He righted himself. "Beg pardon, did I tread upon your toes?"

"Nay. But wot startled ye?"

He had been a fool to believe himself in love withi Arabelle. It wasn't Arabelle's sweet, innocent features that had his heart stuttering; it was this beautiful, enigmatic woman in his arms. At Emma's tired but piercing look, he stepped back and released her. "It's late." He rushed to pick up his waistcoat and donned it like a shield to protect his heart that was pounding in the middle of his chest.

"If ye aren't gonna be honest with me, ye better tell yer brother in the morn that there will be no more lessons."

By god, this woman was fearless and direct. "For a moment, I lost my mind."

"How?"

Honesty was the best policy. "I was confused."

She crossed her arms over her chest and tapped her right forefinger.

"I briefly thought you were someone else."

"Who?"

"Lady Arabelle, Lord Hereford's little sister."

Her finger stopped, and she hugged herself tight. "Do ye fancy Lady Arabelle?"

"No."

She marched over to his discarded greatcoat and hat,

picked them up, and shoved them into his chest. "But ye did once?

"Aye."

She walked over to the door and swiftly unlocked the latches. "There's nothing the matter with yer mind." She swung the door open, letting the frigid night air in. She nodded for him to exit, and he stepped through the threshold. On the stoop, he turned. Emma's sad eyes stunned him.

Using the door as a barrier, she peeked her head around. "Lady Arabelle's grandfather is me sire. There ye have it. I'm a bastard, so I'll not be expectin' ye to return."

The door slid into its frame. The rusty lock clicked into place, followed by two more.

Mute and confused, he stared at the faint firelight that peeked through the weathered wood panel and door frame until it disappeared.

A Hereford sired Emma. It stood to reason she would share some physical similarities to Lady Arabelle, but it didn't explain the undeniable effect Emma had on his mind and body.

Swiveling to face the road, he fought the urge to bang on the door and demand Emma let him in. Spying the whites of two sets of eyes across the way, he stuffed his hands in his coat and began to trudge through the unfamiliar streets on the east end of town. Three blocks from Emma's shop, he still was debating the soundness of his decision to leave.

A hack rolled to a stop next to him. "Me lord, ye look lost. Can I offer ye me assistance?"

"Neale & Sons on the upper west end." He hopped in and huddled in the corner as his mind raced. The coachman was right. He was lost. Emma had him discombobulated, but for the first time in months, he felt alive.

CHAPTER FIVE

*E*mma glanced down the cobbled alley, ensuring no one was about. Wiping her hands over her skirts, she inhaled deeply and scratched at the back door of the offices of Neale & Sons. As the door swooshed open, Emma straightened her spine and walked in without waiting to be invited in. The staff was accustomed to her appearing at irregular times to visit with Bronwyn and no longer escorted Emma to her friend's office. She swiftly marched down the hall to avoid detection by the man who had kept her awake most of the night, briskly opened the door, and sank back against the solid wood as the latch fell into place.

Bronwyn's quill stilled, and she looked up from the parchment. "I wasn't expecting you today."

"Me mum sent me." Emma pushed away from the door. Her heart pounded as if she had been chased despite having evaded Mr. Neale in his own offices. What could explain her ridiculous behavior? For years she'd entered the establishment without having run into him. Why would today be any different? Blast the man for introducing devilish thoughts of sinful kisses and rekindling hopes of love. Egad—she was losing her mind. Love, indeed.

Giving herself a good shake, she firmly planted both hands on Bronwyn's desk and glared at her best friend. "Ye should have told me yerself. But oh no, ye let me spend an entire afternoon sitting on yer posh settee, and ye didn't utter a word about bein' with child."

Emma straightened at her dearest friend's dark stare and crossed her arms—protecting her from any more stabs to the heart Bronwyn might inflict. Her bleedin' best friend hadn't shared the news with her directly. Instead, she'd heard it from her mum, who had learned of Bronwyn's condition through the Network servant channels. The Elders' Council orders were for Emma to persuade Bronwyn to slow down and not overdo in her condition.

"I was advised that nothing was certain until I was further along. *And* you can share with the Elders that unless the midwife advises that my sitting behind a desk is hazardous to the health of the babe, I shall continue to assist Christopher until he finds a suitable replacement."

Emma wanted to stomp her foot. They'd been friends since they were but five years old and hadn't kept a secret from one another since they first met. How could Bronwyn calmly sit there and pretend nothing was amiss? They used to talk about everything. Emma infused all the emptiness, hurt, and rage into her voice.

"*But* the midwife did say ye should take it easy. Ye're carryin' the blasted future Head PORF, for goodness sake!"

"Why are you yelling?" Bronwyn put her quill down and stood. "I know you far too well. When you are angry, you torture me with silence. So out with it. What is truly the matter?"

"I've been ordered here to gain yer promise that ye will have yer replacement in place by week's end." Bronwyn's knowing eyes narrowed, but Emma refused to squirm.

"Did you even attempt to argue my case?"

"Of course I did. I talked until me face was red. They're not askin' ye to lie about. There are three wise women on the council. All have birthed their fair share of bubs, and they know how tirin' it is at the beginning and the end. All they ask is that ye take it easy for now."

Slumping back into the chair, Bronwyn replied, "I don't have the final decision. Christopher does. I can only present him with the best candidates available, and it is up to him to choose who he will hire."

This is how things should be between them. Sorting out their problems together. "Blimey, then I'll have to hunt down yer husband and ask him to advise his brother that if Mr. Neale doesn't choose, someone else will on his behalf."

Bronwyn jumped out of her seat and rounded the desk to wrap Emma in a bear hug. "Good gracious. Please share with me what is the matter with you?"

Pushing her friend away for the first time ever, Emma said, "Stop yer fussin'. There nothin' wrong with me."

"Emma Lennox." Bronwyn grabbed Emma squarely by the upper arms. "You never seek out help from others." Staring eye to eye, Bronwyn continued, "Something has happened. Did Christopher..."

At the mention of his name Emma broke down, and a tear escaped. "Christopher kissed me. *Me.* And then I had to tell him...I told him the truth." Her mouth soured even now at the thought of speaking of her horrid sire. "I'd rather sip arsenic than have to repeat wot I admitted to Mr. Neale. Ye know that."

Bronwyn ushered Emma to the pair of leather chairs separated by a small, round table. Emma sank into one while Bronwyn dragged the other around so that they could sit facing each other.

"Ye shouldn't be movin' the bleedin' furniture about." Emma found her hands being squeezed by her best friend.

"I didn't become some fragile creature as soon as I conceived. Enough about me, please tell me what happened."

"'Tis not much to share. He mistakenly kissed me thinkin' I was Lady Arabelle. I told him the truth—that I was her grandfather's bastard. End of story."

"What do you mean he mistook you for Arabelle?"

"I've heard breedin' causes a woman to lose her wits." Emma raised an eyebrow. "Another fine reason to remain unwed."

"I'm serious, Emma. Why did you allow Christopher to kiss you? You never let your guard down."

She shrugged. She didn't know the answer despite having thought about it all night. She needed to make her escape soon before Bronwyn suspected she might actually fancy Christopher. "I came here to extract a promise from you, and I've a dozen orders waiting, so let me have it."

Bronwyn's lips thinned into a straight line. "I have a better idea. *We* will discuss the matter directly with Christopher."

Emma clenched her fists. There was no way she was going to see Christopher willingly despite the awakening passion he'd exposed. She was no ninny and had her pride. He hadn't been thinking of her when he bent his head to press his lips to hers. He'd imagined it was Lady Arabelle.

There were no secrets among the Network. Her mum preyed upon at the tender age of fourteen by the lecherous old geezer, Ulysses Risley, who was Lord Hereford at the time. Ulysses died before Emma was born, succeeded by his son, Harold, who restored honor to the title at war but also gave his life for his country. The current Lord Hereford, Sebastian, who was watched closely by the Network and PORFs, had thankfully inherited none of his grandfather's terrible traits and continued to honorably uphold the earldom his papa had worked so hard to restore.

From a young age, Emma knew she was different from her siblings. No one in the Network brought up the topic of her lineage. They cared naught, for Emma had also worked hard to prove she had not inherited her sire's villainous tendencies. She didn't fear gossip. The ton's insults couldn't hurt her more than she allowed them to. She refused to let them hurt her or her mum further. The ton didn't scare her. It was her own blasted reactions to Christopher she didn't comprehend.

Bronwyn rose and stood in front of Emma, blocking her from leaving. The door to Bronwyn's office opened moments later, and Mr. Neale's warm tenor voice filled the room. "I've already considered Mr. Brentworth and Mr. Neatherton's applications. Neither of them..." He paused as he peered around Bronwyn and caught a glimpse of Emma. "Beg pardon. I didn't know you had company."

Bronwyn stepped to the side, and Emma rose. If she didn't face Christopher as brazenly as her friend would expect, there would be more prying questions from the only other woman who knew her as well as her mum.

Quickly organizing her thoughts, Emma said, "Mr. Neale, the lack of progress in yer search for Bronwyn's replacement is concernin' given her delicate condition."

"Exactly why I prioritized the matter and am here." He looked her over and smirked. "Are you here to apply for the position?"

"Gor, wot a horrible idea. Absolutely not."

"Shame." Christopher reached into his breast coat pocket and retrieved a letter that he held out for her. "Fortunate that you are here, and I can pass this along to you personally."

Instead of accepting the parchment, she stared at it as if it might bite her. "Wot is it?"

"The instructions for this eve's lessons." His eyes twinkled with mischief.

"I thought I was quite clear last eve. There will be no more lessons."

"I'd hoped you would change your mind."

"Emma never changes her mind, even when she's wrong," Bronwyn chimed in.

Emma turned back to face Bronwyn. "Me sources say if I decline the first gentleman's offer to dance, I'm not allowed to dance with another. Is that the rule?"

Bronwyn sighed. "Aye. You are correct. I hoped you might meet a gentleman who might finally be of interest to you."

Christopher's smile disappeared as his posture stiffened. Ignoring his strange reaction, Emma countered, "Ha. I know ye, Bronwyn Cadby Neale. Ye just want me to join yer misery."

Placing the instructions upon the small table next to her, Christopher said, "I require the use of your office—to speak with Emma, alone."

Bronwyn slid her gaze to Emma. Attempting to appear undaunted, she nodded.

"I'll go order us a pot of tea." Her best friend backed out of the room, her gaze never leaving Emma.

Once the door was shut, Emma opened her mouth, but Christopher raised a hand in the air and said, "I have a proposition."

Her hackles rose at the word proposition. Christopher was a gentleman; certainly he meant nothing untoward. Emma tilted her head and waited for the man to continue.

Christopher continued, "I shall promise to decide upon and hire an assistant the day we satisfactorily finish our dance lessons."

"I already explained. I don't plan on dancing at Bronwyn's ball." She clasped her hands behind her back and added, "There is no need for the lessons nor for those." She nodded towards the white parchment.

"I look forward to your concerned visits when Bronwyn continues to act as my secretary for another few months." He turned as if he was about to leave.

Bloomin' barrister! Emma should have known to tread more carefully in her dealings with him. "Wait."

He swiveled slowly with a smirk that impulsively she wanted to kiss away. "Yes?"

"Five days."

Retrieving the instructions, he stepped closer and opened the parchment. After he scanned its contents, he crisply folded it in half. "If you abide by everything outlined, I believe it possible to complete our lessons in five days, but it will require two or more hours of your time each evening." She reached for the lesson plan, but he held it overhead. "You have to trust me and agree first."

"Ye expect me to trust ye?"

"If you don't trust me, what use is a promise to make an offer of employment five days henceforth?"

It was a clever argument. She didn't trust men. But

Mr. Neale made her want to throw caution to the wind, and his smile made her contemplate wicked things she'd heard whispers about and never experienced in real life.

His lips twitched, but he didn't reveal the smile that she couldn't resist. Instead, he smirked and said, "If you fail to complete the lessons, then I..."

"I won't." She jutted out her chin and stared into his eyes.

Clear, intelligent eyes that begged the question as to why a perceptive man like Christopher would agree to remain unmarked. Now was her chance to find out the answer. "If I agree, ye need to hire Bronwyn's replacement, but ye also agree to receive the mark within the week."

Christopher's eyes narrowed and pinned her with a look that would intimidate most but instead sent a hum of energy through her. "Hmm. Do you know the stipulations my brother has made in regards to the PORF mark being placed upon my body?"

"Aye." Everyone in the Network was aware—he must marry first.

His gaze didn't waver. "Then you must know your demand is unreasonable. Banns would need to be read... And who would you suggest I marry?"

"Ye seem rather fond of Lady Arabelle. Why not procure a special license and propose?" A pang of hurt stabbed at her heart.

He blinked slowly and released a deep sigh. "She is in love with another."

"Blimey, wot does love have anythin' to do with marriage?"

"I want to marry for love like family has before me—my papa, my brother, and even my dear cousin Theo. I will not break the family tradition."

She shifted her weight slightly forward, close enough to poke him in the chest, but she didn't dare touch him. "So ye choose love over duty."

"My wish is that I shall accomplish both, just as both Landon and Theo have."

She stared at him mutely. His answer made no sense, yet he was correct. Both his brother and cousin had successfully managed to find love and fulfill their duties to the Crown. Unable to formulate a witty response, she said, "It is important to both PORFs and the Network that Bronwyn and the babe are hale and safe. I'll settle for your terms. Five days of dance lessons, and ye will no longer require Bronwyn's assistance." She stuck out her hand, expecting him to give her the list of instructions.

Ignoring her hand, he leaned in close and said, "Shall we seal the agreement with a kiss?"

His eyes blazed with interest and settled upon her lips. He wanted to kiss her. It made no sense. She wanted him to want to kiss her, but she suspected he was merely attracted to her looks, so similar to the woman he really wanted. Did she dare take advantage and allow a kiss, knowing it wasn't real?

Her throat tightened, and she croaked, "Do ye kiss men when ye enter deals with them?"

"No." He chuckled, and his lips barely brushed over

the tops of her cheeks as he leaned in to whisper in her ear, "I look forward to our lesson later this eve." He straightened, placed the parchment between her fingers, and left her looking at the door like a pea goose.

Bronwyn returned with a maid laden with a tea tray. Emma tucked the parchment into a hidden pocket within her skirts.

Bronwyn resumed her seat and waited for the young maid to leave her office. The second they were alone again, she asked, "Did he try to kiss you again?"

"Aye." Exhausted both mentally and physically, Emma fell back into her own seat.

"And did you let him a second time?"

"Nay." She fidgeted with her skirts before meeting Bronwyn's questioning gaze. "How is Christopher to receive the mark if he won't marry but for love?"

"Hmm. You didn't grant him a kiss, but you have taken to referring to him by his Christian name. Emma, what are you not telling me?"

"I'm not the one keeping secrets from their best friend."

"I should never have taught you the art of counter-arguments. You are far too good at them." Bronwyn poured the tea and handed Emma her cup.

Accepting the warm drink, Emma pondered Christopher's reasons for continuing the dance lessons. Likely he was afraid of informing Lord Hadfield he'd failed as a dance master. Emma snorted at the thought he simply wished to see her again. To kiss her once more.

"Emma Lennox, whatever it is you are thinking, I caution you to act with care."

Bronwyn was right. She'd have to keep her fanciful thoughts in line and keep her head out of the clouds. Christopher Neale's lessons were for one purpose only—to ensure Emma wouldn't make a fool of herself at Bronwyn's debut ball.

CHAPTER SIX

*C*hristopher's hands rose from the ivory keys as the last notes of the haunting and somber piece reverberated through his body. He'd specifically chosen the monstrosity of a townhouse as his bachelor lodging for its proximity to Neale & Sons offices and the music room that accommodated his grand piano. The musical instrument was his first purchase that had no other purpose but his own pleasure.

In Landon's first year as earl, Christopher had dutifully overseen the renovations to the dilapidated townhome his brother had inherited and had remained until Bronwyn's arrival. After living at Hadfield townhouse, surrounded by dwellings owned by other hereditary lords for two long years, he finally had extracted himself from the prying eyes of the ton. The move to his own lodging hadn't come soon enough for his taste. Raised in a modest residence befitting their papa's station as a well-respected barrister, Christopher chose the lower west end of London, closer to their childhood neighborhood.

Playing and composing always eased his mind and assisted him in sorting out his often tumultuous emotions. His dealings with Emma were unsettling. Her self-assured demeanor both captivated and confounded him. He speculated that she too questioned her place in life. As the natural daughter of the current Lord Hereford's grandfather, she was half-aunt to Lady Arabelle. As presumptive heir to Landon's title, Christopher was left questioning his position in the world. Not a peer. A gentleman stuck in between two worlds—that of the working gentry and the ton. Required to attend countless mind-numbing social events amid lords and ladies, Christopher had begun seeking out the kind, sweet Lady Arabelle. Forging a bond of friendship with the lady had been relatively easy. And while he had considered proposing marriage, he never once experienced the skin tingling, heart-thumping sensations Emma had evoked during their two brief meetings. Emma emitted an under-current of energy that sparked emotions he had previously only believed existed in poetry. It was these rampaging feelings that had led him to devise an elaborate plan for this eve's dance lesson. Plans that required his mama's assistance.

The chime of the longcase clock from the adjacent drawing room marked the time for him to prepare for his mama and Emma's arrival. Inhaling and exhaling slowly, he stretched out his back with hands clasped above his head. But the excitement of seeing Emma again awakened every nerve in his body. The patter of his mama's quick, decisive steps approaching had him closing his eyes and sending a prayer up to his maker that by the end of the evening, Emma would be a willing participant in the lessons and as eager to see him as he was to see her again. He opened his eyes as the music room doors opened.

Christopher stood and crossed the room to greet his guests.

His mama placed her hands on his cheeks and pulled his face down to meet hers. "Dear boy, you work too hard. You're looking rather weary." She patted his cheek with her right hand and then turned to Emma. "Never fear, we shall practice the waltz tonight. Perhaps the less vigorous French version."

Emma nodded. Her pale yellow gown complemented her eyes, making them appear more green than blue this evening. As his mama made her way to the pianoforte, he bowed and asked, "May I have this dance?"

Emma placed her hand in his. "Since I won't have been formally introduced to the gentlemen at the ball, I suppose I'll only have to agree to dance with you."

Straightening to his full height, he smiled. Oddly, her statement evoked feelings of both sympathy and possessiveness simultaneously. "I am certain there will be a great number of men seeking an introduction, and I wager your dance card will be filled within an hour of your arrival."

"Why?"

His mama tapped upon a few keys. "Wonderful." She

smiled and captured his full attention. "I was worried you spent too much time in the office and had neglected this beauty. Shall we begin?" Without waiting for a reply, she began playing a Mozart-inspired melody.

Emma was the first to act. Under the layers of clothing, his skin tingled as her free hand moved up his chest, along the top of his shoulder, behind his neck. Her movements halted.

"Ye are too tall. Me arm..." Emma withdrew and pulled back, waving her freed hands in the air. "Yer drawings showed the woman's arm..."

Christopher chuckled. "I apologize; my illustrations did not account for the variance in our heights. We shall have to make modifications."

The music stopped, and his mama asked, "What are the two of you chattering about?" She rose and strode to stand before him and Emma. "I'll not be sitting over there playing my heart out while you two squabble. Now, what is the matter?"

"Yer son's instructions were all wrong," Emma answered before he could. She was fast to act and straight to the point. It was a refreshing quality in a woman.

His mama turned to face him. "Pray explain?"

"I merely provided Emma with a few drawings of the various positions we will assume while..."

His mama's raised eyebrows made him pause. "Is that so?" His mama was the only other living soul that knew of his passion for music and drawing, both of which he'd abandoned these two years past, busy with running the firm Landon had left to him to oversee.

His mama's gaze switched between him and Emma before settling on Emma. "When did he give them to you?"

"This morn, Aunt Henri."

Christopher looked from Emma to his mama and back again. "Aunt Henri?"

His mama continued as if he'd not spoken. "And you have studied them all."

"Aye."

She wrapped Emma in a warm hug. "I've always been fond of you, girl, but now you have my heart." She leaned back and said, "Promise to be patient with him."

What was his mama on about?

Averting his attention back to Emma, he said, "Shall we try again?"

"Have ye decided upon Bronwyn's replacement?"

She was persistent. He'd give her that. He hid the grin that he rarely shared with anyone but family and said, "No." He placed her right hand in his left. "However, I have selected five candidates, and I intend to eliminate one each day as we progress through our lessons."

She didn't hesitate. Emma positioned her left hand out in front of her and turned so that they stood hip to hip. He admired her courage and determination. But what he really wanted to see was if he could recreate the interest in her gaze from the night before. Which would be an impossible task with his talented mama seated at the pianoforte watching with them with peripheral vision only mothers possess. From the moment she entered the music room, Emma had carefully avoided his gaze—he'd be lucky to coax forth a smile. Damnation. His stroke of brilliance to have his mama chaperone for the evening to protect Emma from scandal and horrid gossip was, in fact, a deucedly ill-conceived plan.

He glanced over at his mama and nodded. With a wink and a smile, his mama placed her fingers over the keys, ready to begin.

Christopher bent his head down and said, "Perhaps you can rest your arm along my back." She placed her arm about his waist, which felt natural but wouldn't do in public. "Slightly higher so that your arm is straight." He let his hand brush along the back of her neck as his hand came to rest upon her shoulder. Her whole body shuddered. He looked down at her, but her lips were drawn tight and her gaze trained in front of them.

As the music began, Christopher led Emma through the marche, and they smoothly transitioned into the pirouette position—facing one another, gazes locked, her right hand in his. Finally, he saw the spark he'd been fixated upon all day.

Emma said, "What're ye grinnin' about?"

"Am I smiling?"

"Aye. But I'd rather ye be not foolin' yerself. I'm not Lady Arabelle."

He frowned. "I've not lost my senses. I'm fully aware of who I have in my arms." He narrowed his gaze as they slid into a more intimate position, his foot between hers. With the barest of pressure, he squeezed her hand before he raised their joined hands to make an arc above her head. Turning ever so slowly, he simply stared into her eyes.

"Are ye goin' to make conversation now, or is it the woman's duty to start the idle chatter?"

He had forgotten himself, imaging he was dancing with a woman who wanted to dance with him, not one who had been coerced to spend time with him.

"Miss Lennox, are you looking forward to the ball?"

Emma pasted a wide smile on her face, but it didn't erase the scrunch of her brow. "Bronwyn ordered me to be present. I'll never disobey a direct order from a PORF."

No, Emma wouldn't dishonor the oath she took. She was more likely to devise a scheme that would allow her to avoid such orders in the future, though. "I can't imagine you like letting others order you about."

Puffing out her chest, Emma said, "It's a great honor to serve and protect the PORFs. Me family has done so for generations. Bronwyn may have been me friend first, but she's a PORF now and married to the Head PORF at that."

He glanced over to see his mama happily lost in the music. He bent his head and asked the question that had plagued him. "Are you at all worried?"

He'd changed topics without preamble, but the recognition in Emma's eyes was clear.

Not skipping a beat, she easily matched his steps as they promenaded about the room. "Ye're asking if I care if the ton notices or figures out me connection to the Herefords."

"Yes." The brush of her skirts against his leg sent his thoughts scattering for a moment before his gaze landed back upon her serious features.

"I can't change who me sire was. And I'm not attendin' for me own pleasure. I'm there to support Bronwyn." She twisted at the waist to face him. Her brow wrinkled with concern. "Do ye fink me presence will look poor upon Bronwyn?"

Her question poked a hole in his heart. She wasn't concerned even a little for herself but was troubled by the embarrassment her appearance might cause for her best friend. She was remarkably strong-willed. Uncertain how best to answer, Christopher squeezed her hand that remained securely in his.

Turning her, so she was face-to-face with him once more, he said, "I confess, the inner workings of the ton are far beyond me. I'd hope Theo would have advised Bronwyn and you if it were to be a problem."

Her features relaxed at the mention of his cousin Theo. "Brilliant. I'll jus' have to remember to ask Lady Theo for her opinion tomorrow."

"What will you do if Theo says you should not attend?"

She pursed her lips in thought. Christopher was quickly becoming fond of the habit. With a smile, Emma answered, "First, I'll send ye a note lettin' ye know I'll not have to continue with these bloomin' lessons. Second, I'll simply track Bronwyn down and tell her how it is. I'll not bring shame upon her or Lord Hadfield."

He liked her smiling, and so he teased, "Oh, Landon

will be so disappointed to hear you still refer to him by his title."

"He's the bloomin' Head PORF. Of course I'll refer to him with respect."

She made him smile, and he wasn't about to release her from their agreement. "You can't quit. The deal was five dance lessons under my tutelage, and in return, I shall hire an assistant. The lessons were never dependent upon you attending the ball."

She stopped mid-twirl. "Ye're tryin' to confuse me, spinnin' me around and yammerin' on like a lawyer. If ye fink I shouldn't go, then why did ye insist on these silly lessons?"

He told her the truth. "I wanted to spend time with you and dance with you."

"Why—because I remind ye of Lady Arabelle? If ye can't have 'er, ye want to dally with me?"

"Yes. No." He didn't release her. "Wait, let me explain."

She raised a pretty eyebrow, detangled herself from him, and crossed her arms. If he peeked under her skirts, he'd probably see her tapping her foot, but she remained stock still, and there was no sound to indicate he was right.

He needed her back in his arms. His mama played on, blissfully unaware that they had stopped dancing. Placing his hand on the small of her back, he inched closer and brought his hand up just below her chin. He dared not to touch her until he'd fully explained. "This has nothing to do with Lady Arabelle. She made her choice, and the woman chose another. I made the deal... well, I'm not certain of why except that I couldn't focus on anything but counting the minutes until I'd see you again."

Emma's shoulder's relaxed a tad at his ill-formulated explanation. On a half sigh, she said, "Thank ye for yer honesty. If Lady Theo deems it unwise for me to attend the ball, I shall send word as I've no interest in prancin' about when I've orders to fill. If I do have to attend, then I'll ask ye simply send over more of yer drawings."

Her rejection stung. He lifted her chin up, so she had no choice but to meet his gaze. "Is it really a torture to spend an evening with me?"

The chit rolled her eyes. "Do ye know how long it takes to design, cut patterns and material, and sew one gown for these women?" She stripped off her gloves. "It takes a few hundred pinpricks and at least three days of sewin', and I've got orders up to me eyeballs."

He wasn't going to give up the chance to spend more time with Emma. "Illustrations are not enough. I'll compromise; if you are to attend, I shall provide the drawings, and I'll give you tomorrow night as a reprieve, but we must meet the following eve."

Eyes narrowed, she searched his features. With a curt nod that dislodged his touch, she said, "Agreed."

He released the air trapped in his lungs. "I shall eagerly await to hear my dear cousin's verdict tomorrow."

Emma left him and walked straight up to his mama without a second glance at him. She tapped his mama's shoulder, and the music came to a jarring halt.

"Sorry, Aunt Henri. I didn't mean to startle you."

His mama smiled and flickered her gaze over at him. "Had enough of my son already?"

"Aye."

Emma treated his mama with a level of deference she didn't take with him. In fact, she treated both Bronwyn and Landon with the same level of respect. Yet, she treated him entirely differently. Uncertain if he was irritated by the fact or pleased, he escorted the women to the coach with the Hadfield crest awaiting them out front.

CHAPTER SEVEN

*E*mma arranged her skirts as Aunt Henri retrieved and passed her a blanket from a hidden compartment under the opposite bench. "What displeases you about my son?"

Nothing got past this woman.

Emma sighed. "Why did you and your husband decide not to have your children receive the mark at birth?"

"Simple. My dear belated husband, in his infinite wisdom, believed that the mark shapes a man's thinking before he can form his own identity. He wanted our sons to be free to decide their fate." She smiled. "I see you do not agree with my late husband's logic."

The coach rattled along the cobbled streets mimicking Emma's thoughts. "It is an honor, not a burden."

"And is that the sentiment you hold towards being born into a Network that serves PORFs?"

"What has Lord Hadfield shared with you about the Network?"

"Child, you could have been my own daughter, answering questions with a question just like my boys." Aunt Henri smiled and answered, "Naught. But I sense he has ruffled a few feathers amongst the Network."

"In choosing Bronwyn for wife, he stirred a pot that had been simmerin' for a long while. Lord Hadfield is astute and has a way about him that we are comin' to understand. He's nothing like his brother."

"Oh, I think you might have underestimated my younger son. Christopher is, in fact, more akin to his papa —unassuming but extremely hard to deter once they've set their course."

Hmph. Christopher appeared quite happy to adhere to his older brother's wishes and happily run the family business. Yet there had been a time or two when Emma noted the extra moment Christopher took to answer particular questions and sensed the silent sighs when he was torn between his own desires and those he cared for and respected. Christopher might not be the man she had initially assumed him to be.

"I don't think Christopher has decided upon a future."

Aunt Henri burst into laughter. "Oh my dear child, he most definitely has already chosen a path on which to venture. And in typical Christopher fashion, it is not an easy route."

She patted Emma on the knee and promptly closed her eyes, leaving Emma a tad befuddled. Emma ran her sweaty hands over her skirts, pausing at the spot where Aunt Henri had touched her in a motherly fashion. Emma refrained from poking the woman to demand what in the blazes she believed her son was up to. Aunt Henri was a PORF, and Emma needed to remember that fact, irrespective of how the woman treated her. From the very first time they met, Aunt Henri had treated Emma as family. A bond Emma valued and did not wish to risk.

The corner of Aunt Henri's lips remained curved in a slight grin. What was so amusing? The woman's smile disappeared, her eyes popped wide open as she righted herself straight as a pole. "Hereford and Landon have been rather cozy lately. If my intuition is correct, you won't be able to continue hiding from Lord Hereford. Your half-nephew is an extremely honorable and determined young fellow. I suspect he will figure some way to claim you as family."

"I've been thinkin' upon it...and just this eve your son brought up another matter I need to seek Theo's counsel on."

"Oh?"

"Do ye fink it wise for Bronwyn to be associated with me in front of her new peers? Will me presence harm her chances of formin' strong and good bonds with the ladies of the ton?"

"I was disowned by my own papa, a duke no less, for marrying a second son. Yet the women I once called friends have once again welcomed me back into their fold. Bronwyn will have to be brave and learn how to navigate the social whirl, and she has wonderful instincts in whom to trust."

"Ye mean she doesn't trust anyone."

"Exactly. But I will defer to my wise young niece as to your question. I wish it were a simple matter and I could advise you that the views and opinions of the ton do not matter, but in reality, not only is Bronwyn now a countess, she is also the wife to the Head PORF, which means there are far more implications to consider."

"Aye. I'd not want to embarrass or bring scandal upon Bronwyn." The plush squabs of the Hadfield coach beneath her thighs were reminders of her best friend's new life as Countess Hadfield.

"Let's wait to discuss with Theo. She has a mind for considering all the consequences."

"Will you be accompanyin' her to her fitting?"

"I hadn't planned on doing so, but perhaps I should. Would you like me to be there?"

Emma tensed every muscle. She was to do the bidding of PORFs, not the other way around. "Only if it is yer wish."

Clack. Aunt Henri struck the heel of her foot hard against the coach floor. "Child, you'd best become comfortable speaking your mind with me, or I'll not have you for a daughter-in-law."

Emma whipped her head to face Aunt Henri. "Why would ye say something so half-cocked?"

"I saw the way Christopher looked at you tonight. He's already half in love with you."

"Nay. He's not. Christopher's in love with Lady Arabelle, and sometimes he gets us mixed up, is all."

"Are you certain?" Aunt Henri's eyebrows arched upwards. "I've seen him dance with Lady Arabelle on a number of occasions, and I can attest it was not at all the same."

"Yer son is a gentleman, and as soon as he weds, he'll become an official PORF. I'll be honor-bound to serve."

The coach swayed to the right as they made a turn. Emma righted herself as Aunt Henri mumbled, "Oh, you'll be bound to honor him if he has anything to do with it."

Egad. Emma adored the woman, but Aunt Henri was delusional—Christopher wasn't in love or plotting to wed her. Her heart raced a little faster. Aunt Henri was no fool and seldom wrong.

"Do you not find my son desirable?"

Oh, she found Christopher to be alluring...captivating, and extremely attractive. Clear images of Christopher dressed only in his lawn shirt and trousers increased her body temperature and brought a pink tinge to her cheeks. She could only hope her bodily reactions were masked in the dimly lit coach.

"My lady, ye birthed two incredibly handsome men, one with a dimple that hazes the mind and the other with a smile that blinds a woman. But I'm not one to dally about with a man, and I'm quite certain Christopher would not want to marry a woman like me, sired out of wedlock and all."

"You don't think much of Christopher then." Disappointment settled into the fine lines around Aunt Henri's eyes, making her appear older than she usually did.

How was she to explain? While her sire had unexplainably fathered an honorable heir, who sired one also, she was conceived from a horrific experience. Bad blood flowed through her veins. She never wanted to taint her family or any other. Emma tried her best to live without reproach at all times. Had even distanced herself from her loving family, for she had sinful thoughts all the time. Especially when she danced in the arms of the charming Christopher Neale—barrister, gentleman, and future PORF. She experienced a wicked longing to have Christopher's lips upon hers when he melted her heart with his intense gazes. Even knowing he was picturing another lady, she didn't care. She wanted to pretend she was the one he undressed with his eyes.

The coach came to a halt. Emma admitted, "I didn't think much of him before I met him." Crisply folding the blanket and placing it on the rear-facing seat, Emma continued, "But after spending a few hours with him, it's clear he needs a smart, talented woman to wed." A woman who could read books and debate with him in the evenings. Not someone like her who fancied evenings filled with kisses and the pleasure of his glorious taut body next to hers. No. Christopher Neale should marry a woman of equal breeding and intelligence.

The coach door swung open. Aunt Henri said, "We are not done conversing." The footman nodded and closed the door. Capturing Emma's hand, Aunt Henri continued, "What my son deserves is a woman who will love him for his rather confounding and complex personality. As his mother, I assure you it will take an extraordinary woman to tempt my dear son into matrimony."

"He's young. He has time yet."

Aunt Henri let out an unladylike snort. "Not according to Landon. He's advised his brother to find a wife by the end of the season, or he will choose one for him."

Tugging her hand free, Emma asked, "How is it that the Network doesn't know of this edict?"

"Ha. Such a bold question. You would have to become a PORF in order for me to answer. I trust I've not misjudged in confiding in you. You won't share this information, will you?"

"Aunt Henri, yer a sly fox."

The woman winked at her. Continuing her bold actions, Aunt Henri did the unthinkable—she pushed open the door and then Emma out of the carriage.

Emma whirled around before the coach door closed. "Will I see ye later?"

"I don't think so, child. I believe I've given you enough to ponder. I'll leave you in Theo's capable hands."

CHAPTER EIGHT

*B*leary-eyed, Emma ran a finger over the row of stitches that she somehow managed to sew. After another night of restless sleep, she rose and, by candlelight, began to sew, whittling down the mound of work that had amassed due to her lack of concentration over the past two days.

The first streaks of light began to filter through her clean shop windows, followed by the tinkle of the overhead bell. Theo had finally arrived.

Theo was one of the stealthiest of the PORFs. Only her husband rivaled her skill in entering a room undetected. "Good gracious, I've never seen so many gowns in their various states." Theo's sweet authoritative voice just beyond the curtain gave away the woman's position in the room.

Bronwyn's soft footsteps meant she too was close by. "No doubt Emma will say it's my fault."

Emma pushed back the curtain, separating the

receiving room from the back. "It *is* yer bloomin' fault. Ye invited too many guests, and I've even had to turn away some clients, for the first time, and I'm not at all happy about it."

"Denying a client or two will only make your dresses more desirable." Theo twirled to face Emma and rushed to her side. "Whatever is the matter? You look dreadful."

"Nothing is the matter. I've not slept much, is all."

Bronwyn came over and felt her forehead. "No fever. Do you want me to summon more help for you?"

Emma huffed. "I don't need ye meddling in my business. It's the silly dance lessons that are taking up too much of me time."

Bronwyn, wide-eyed, replied, "But Christopher said last night's lesson went splendid."

"According to my sources, you have concerns regarding the ball that you wish to discuss with me." Theo stepped up onto the platform and rubbed her rounded belly. "What do you wish to ask?"

"Christopher prompted me to consider the possibility of others noticing and making mention of my lineage. Perhaps my attendance will harm the success of Bronwyn's first ball."

"He has a point. It might be rather awkward for you."

"I don't care about me. I'm worried about Bronwyn."

"I'm sorry; you never seemed to care who knew of your bloodline." Bronwyn clutched her hands. "Forgive me for asking this of you."

"Ye know I don't give a farthin' wot the ton or others fink of me, so ye don't need to be apologizin'."

Theo spoke up. "Your lack of care hasn't resulted in harm to date due to the fact you've been able to remain in the shadows...and Hereford has respected your decision. But Lady Arabelle has not been as covert as her brother, claiming she will only wear gowns designed by her reclusive aunt and sewn exclusively by your shop."

"Eek. *Aunt* makes me sound ancient."

Bronwyn said, "You're only four years her senior."

"That's not the point," Theo said. "Lord Hereford and Lady Arabelle have been without parental guidance for many years. Neither adheres to the strict parameters the ton expects. The fact is, your niece is proud of you, and if you appear, Lady Arabelle will no doubt claim you as family, and you will no longer be able to remain in the shadows. It is your choice, but once you come out of hiding, there is no going back. You will obviously have the support of your most loyal clientele, and of course, you will have our full support. But it is a life-changing decision. You should consider it very carefully."

Emma turned to Bronwyn; best friend or not, she was sworn to abide by the woman's wishes. "What do you wish for me to do?"

"I want what is best for you and your future. When I selfishly asked, I secretly wished you would meet and fall in love with one of the gentlemen at the ball, and you could join me in the endless rounds of tea and terrible biscuits."

"What would ye know of days of tea and biscuits? Ye spend yer days at Neale & Sons with Christopher."

Bronwyn and Theo's eyes widened at her use of

Christopher's first name. Bronwyn said, "You sound jealous."

"Ye two are PORFs. Ye are supposed to tell me wot you wish, and I shall obey, not tell me to do whatever I wish. It's not the way of things."

"It will be going forward. Landon wishes for a more collaborative relationship between PORFs and the Network, and Theo fully supports her cousin."

Emma busied herself, pinning another panel to Theo's expanding waistline. The two PORFs discussed Landon's plans—plans to change the way things had been done for generations. But Emma liked the way things were. They were definitely not perfect, but she knew her place. For decades, the distinction between PORFs and Network members had worked, even if it was dysfunctional. Emma detested change.

As Bronwyn and Theo prepared to leave, Bronwyn said, "If you decide not to come, I fully support your decision. If you decide to come, it will be an honor to have you stand next to me. Either way, you'll not be rid of me as your best friend." She wrapped Emma in a hug, and when she pulled back, she tugged on a loose tendril of hair like they used to as girls. It was a reminder of how close they had been, and even after Bronwyn's station changed, her best friend still treated her the same.

Theo embraced her next. "I, too, fully support your decision whatever you choose."

They left. Emma turned the sign in the window to closed and sank to the settee. How was she to decide what was best?

CHAPTER NINE

*C*hristopher's heart sank as he closed and locked the door behind the last employee to leave. Returning to his office, usually a refuge from his confounding personal life, Christopher slumped into his chair, hands cradling the back of his head. The stack of files awaiting his attention remained piled high. With no word from Emma, he lacked the concentration to study the necessary case law to ensure his clients victory in the courtroom. He missed reviewing the complex trade agreements that had, in recent years, extended to transatlantic dealings. Drafting and negotiating multifaceted terms for British importers provided him an outlet for his legal skills but also harnessed his talent to foresee the other party's intent and next move. Theo shared his abilities and was lucky enough to have found an outlet to fully utilize her skills as wife to the Home Secretary.

Leaning forward, he snatched up his quill and reached for a clean piece of parchment. He should have pressed Bronwyn for answers. But he wanted to hear from Emma.

He dipped the tip of the quill into the ink well, and an unnerving sensation of doom settled into his chest. The nib scratched against the parchment. For years, his ability to recreate a person's likeness had been stifled, but the lines on the page were flowing through him with ease. An outline Emma's now familiar profile and supple body was coming to life. Damnation. Of all the people of his acquaintance, his sister-in-law's brash friend had to be the one to become his muse.

Lady Arabelle had pricked his interest in music, but Emma had ignited his desire to draw and compose. From an early age, his appreciation for the human form meant his gaze was drawn to beautiful women. He was no saint, and he freely admitted to having shared a bed with a charming lady or two who had managed to catch his attention over the years. But not only did Emma capture his attention, she had seized his every thought and was slowly seeping into his heart. He caught himself humming as he finished the drawing.

Emma's beguiling image stared back at him. This was no mere infatuation with a pretty face and lush body. No, Emma evoked a primal need within him to explore and possess her. Damnation, it was more. He didn't want to simply possess her. He wanted her to want him in return. Hoped that she too experienced this magnetism that grew each day. But with each passing moment without a word from Emma, his hope dwindled. He rubbed his weary eyes. The candle had burned down to barely a nub. He pulled out his pocket watch, and the blasted timepiece confirmed it was nearly one in the morn. He should seek out his bed instead of waiting for Emma to magically appear. A shiver of fear tickled the back of his neck. Emma was a woman of her word. He should have heard from her by now. Something was amiss. He bolted for the door, grabbing his hat and coat on his way out.

Christopher nearly ran right into his brother, who was mounting the stairs. "Where are you headed?"

"To see Emma."

"Let's go inside, shall we?"

Landon walked past, leaving Christopher to follow.

"Is all well?" Christopher asked as they entered his office and relit the candle on his desk. "Why are you out and about at this hour?"

Landon moved to pull back the curtain to allow the moonlight into the dim room. Rummaging through his desk drawer, Christopher retrieved two candles and lit those as well, revealing Landon's concerned face.

Landon said, "I invited Emma to dine with us this eve."

"You mean you ordered her."

"Bronwyn was concerned Emma would not eat tonight. My wife also informed me it was you who brought to light the challenges Emma might face."

"Didn't Emma seek out Theo for advice?"

"She did. Emma asked I pass this along to you."

Christopher took the parchment from his brother.

Mr. Neale
Me thanks ye fer yer help, but I no longer need a
dance teacher.
Emma

She didn't need him. Bitter, Christopher said, "Well, she's not one for flowery words."

Landon frowned. "She took extra care to pen the note herself. Bronwyn offered to write it for her, but she refused, stating she needed to tell you herself. It was a huge undertaking for her, and it appears you are not deserving or appreciative of her efforts."

"She runs one of the most sought-after dress shops, and you are telling me she can't write."

"Emma was never taught to read nor write."

"But she has a bookshelf full of books in her store."

"For her patrons' enjoyment." Landon paused, and his eyes fell upon the discarded drafts of Christopher's sketches. Landon raised an eyebrow and asked, "What are those?"

Christopher answered, "Instructions for Emma."

Remarkable. The woman couldn't read, yet she'd interpreted his rather rudimentary drawings, excelling in executing the various positions with ease. The reminder of her in his arms last night reinforced his desire to see her again. But first, he had to be rid of Landon.

His brother continued to stare at sketches with acute interest.

Organizing the papers into a stack, Christopher asked, "Do you agree with her decision?"

"It was Emma's choice. No one involved wants to see her hurt. Least of all Bronwyn." Landon eased into the chair and crossed his legs. Drumming his fingers upon his knee, he continued, "But I admit I was surprised. Emma has the will of an ox, and I'd not thought she cared a whit about what the ton thought of her."

Christopher flipped the top drawing over and clasped his hands on top of them. "So, you suspect she is doing it to protect Bronwyn."

"Or someone she cares about." Landon's fingers stilled. "Why do I get the feeling you are not sharing information?"

"I'm not withholding anything from you."

"The muscle in your right cheek twitched. You are not being entirely honest with me. Mama made some obscure insinuation that you attempted to kiss my wife's dearest friend, but Emma believes it was only due to her resemblance to Lady Arabelle. What say you?"

Christopher took a moment to subdue the urge to lunge across the desk and punch his older brother. "I'm not a rogue going about town debauching innocent women." Releasing a sigh, he added, "I'll admit for a brief moment during our first meeting, I may have been confused by Emma's resemblance to Lady Arabelle. However, I see Emma with such clarity now that there is absolutely no confusing her with another."

"Is that so?" Landon nodded to the illustrations he had been working on. "And those?"

"A medium to expel the images from my mind is all."

"It is your wish to banish Emma from your thoughts?"

"The damn woman is a conundrum. Confounding. Bewitching."

"Sounds to me you have much to consider, little brother." The annoying dent in Landon's cheek appeared as an all-knowing smile formed on his brother's smug face. "Both Bronwyn and I appreciate your attempts to teach Emma how to dance." Narrowing his gaze, Landon added, "Emma did share with me your agreement."

His scheme to spend more time with Emma had failed. "I shall hire an assistant by week's end." If he had a capable secretary in place, it would free his time. Time he could spend getting to know Emma better.

"My thanks, brother." Landon patted one of the large stacks of files upon his desk. "It does appear you are in need of help. Should I return tomorrow?"

"No need." He had everything under control.

Running the family law firm hadn't been his choice, but it was his responsibility nonetheless. He wasn't one to shirk his duties nor disappoint his family. He simply had to resign himself to his lot and ignore the yearning to create something apart from his papa's legacy. Landon had adapted, and so would he.

Landon leisurely rose out of his seat. "Very well. I'll leave you to it and see myself out."

Christopher nodded and waited for Landon's booted footsteps to fade. Picking up the drawings of Emma, he debated whether or not to go see her. The faster he thumbed through the illustrations, the more the woman came to life—a vibrant, independent woman. Emma was right. She didn't need him to teach her a thing. She was perfect in her own right.

Exhaustion settled in—his entire body heavy weighed down by melancholy. He blew out the candles and headed home. The easy jaunt to his townhouse was taxing, as his feet carried him in the opposite direction his heart wished to venture.

PUNCHING HIS PILLOW, Christopher cursed his inability to fall asleep. His conversation with Landon repeated over and over in his mind. His brother naturally asked a great many questions, and even when he had attempted to hide the truth, Landon had simply accepted Christopher's weak responses without further inquisition.

Something was amiss.

Landon had hinted Emma's decision had something to do with protecting someone she cared for and not necessarily Bronwyn. He wouldn't get rest until he had the answer. He rolled out of bed. Early morning sunlight filtered through the curtains as he let his eyes adjust for a moment. Ignoring the clothes that had been neatly laid out by the valet Landon insisted he hire, Christopher entered the adjoining room that housed his clothes. He retrieved a pair of trousers and a simple lawn shirt and made quick work of dressing.

Christopher stood in front of the looking glass. Relocating to a residence of his own hadn't brought with it the independence he'd craved. He loved being close to family, but being an heir to a title and brother to the leader of a clandestine organization were limiting rather than liberating. He'd ignored the constant, watchful, and well-meaning footmen while in residence with Landon, but having another subset watch over his home even though he had yet to receive the mark of a PORF seemed a waste of resources.

Narrowing his gaze at the man in the mirror, Christopher shook his head. Hmph. The man before him appeared the relaxed, nonchalant second son of a gentleman. It was a look he'd mastered, but Christopher's muscles were definitely strained taut beneath his clothing. Christopher's mask had only ever been stripped from him twice. Both times by a brazen, cockney-accented blonde who danced in his arms.

Jamming his arms through his greatcoat sleeves, Christopher strode through his townhouse. He'd nearly made it to the front door.

"Mr. Neale. Mr. Neale," his housekeeper called out from behind him.

He swiveled and waited for the meddling woman to catch up to him. "Yes, Mrs. Gainville."

The woman wiped her hands over her apron. "Mr. Neale...umm..." She threw her hands in the air and said, "She didn't want us to wake ye... She's been waitin' for ye in the kitchens. Of course, ye appear when she popped into...never ye mind about that."

Summoning the last remnants of patience he

possessed, Christopher asked, "It's rather early, as you say, Mrs. Gainville. Pray tell, who is *she*?"

"Miss Emma Lennox, sir."

"Emma?" He stepped away from the front door and headed toward the kitchens.

He entered the warm, herb-scented room. Amidst the busy space, Emma stood by the prep table, chattering away with one of the kitchen hands who was whisking eggs.

Not wanting to interrupt, he took a moment to take in her image. She was beautiful in her day dress – a shade of light blue that reminded him of a cloudless day. It was simple and functional in design, not at all like the walking dresses with bows and flounces favored by the ladies of the ton.

Emma's gaze fell upon him, and Christopher cleared the lump from his throat. "Someone should have seen to your comfort and summoned me."

"I prefer the kitchens, and I've enjoyed chattin' with me friends."

"You came to visit your friends and not me, then."

"Don't be daft; of course, I've come to see ye." A flash of uncertainty crossed her features.

Uncertainty was not a look that suited her. He wanted to see her relaxed and smiling in his home. "Let's adjourn to the morning room, shall we? Mrs. Gainville, a pot of coffee and tea would be wonderful."

"Yes, Mr. Neale, right away." His housekeeper gave Emma a push forward and whispered, "Go on, just tell him."

Emma nodded and replied, "Me thanks for yer ear."

Christopher pretended not to have overheard the brief words between the two and swiveled to lead Emma out of the kitchens.

He opened the door to the sparse morning room, where he normally took his morning meal. In fact, he realized all the rooms in his house lacked the warmth of a woman's presence. Which was highlighted by the energy that trailed Emma as she walked past him.

She walked straight for the window and peered out onto the street. No surprise; Emma had been well trained by the Network to protect its assets. He lacked the mark of a PORF but had slowly accepted the fact that the Network, which had stayed on the fringes of his life as a child, now infiltrated every aspect of his world. Unmarked, he was supposed to be oblivious to the fact his entire household staff were carefully chosen members of the Network, selected to serve and protect him in anticipation of him receiving the mark as soon as he wed. Even as a child, Christopher had noted the subtle protective nature of the Hadfield staff over its masters. And his suspicion that his family was, in fact, one of the three legendary families sworn to protect the royal family was confirmed when Theo fell in love with Lord Archbroke and confessed to having inherited the PORF family volume instead of Landon. Since then, he pretended to not know of Theo and Landon's clandestine schemes, knowing that if either of them needed his assistance, they would simply ask. But as the months went by, it became clear neither would involve him until he officially became a PORF.

Emma turned, and the sunny smile she gifted him banished his gloomy thoughts. He pulled out a chair for Emma. "I trust Mark and David have relieved Paul and Sean."

"How do you know your watches' names?" She slid into the chair.

Leaning down to speak next to her ear, he said, "I have impeccable hearing and a mind for names and schedules."

The scent of lemons caught his attention. But it was the devilish twinkle in her eyes as her gaze slipped to his mouth and then back to his eyes that had his breath catching in his chest.

Scant inches away, Emma twisted her face towards his. Her lips were perfectly aligned with his. The minx's tongue peeked out at the corner of her mouth. She was pure temptation, and he declined to resist. He leaned in closer. A soft moan escaped as their lips touched. The tender kiss was intoxicating, breathtaking. He pulled back. Emma's eyes fluttered open.

Barely louder than a whisper, Christopher said, "I'd like to do that every morn."

Emma's brow creased into a frown. "Every morn?"

Damnation. She had obliterated his self-control. A barrister knew better than to blurt out his thoughts. He stepped away to take a seat at the table. "Please accept my apology. I don't know what caused me to speak without forethought."

Her frown disappeared, and she calmly clasped her hands atop the table.

One of the newly appointed footmen entered and beamed a smile at Emma. It was the first time Christopher had seen the young fellow show any reaction since he appeared within his household. With inherent grace, Emma reached for the pot and poured. Yes, he could quickly become accustomed to her at his table.

"While I am pleased to see you, would you care to share with me the reason for this early morning visit?"

"I came to talk to ye about our agreement."

"I'm listening."

"I need ye to agree to hire an assistant."

"I believe you still owe me the pleasure of your company for three more evenings."

"Me company?" She narrowed her gaze. "Wot ever for?"

When questioned directly, his first mental response was not for the ears of an innocent.

Before he could formulate an appropriate answer, Emma challenged, "Ye don't know, do ye?"

"I know that when you are near, I want to linger." Not the right response.

Emma's frown returned. "Ye can linger with another woman. Me nights are reserved for work."

"I merely meant I enjoy your company. You did agree to..."

"To dance lessons. Not yer heart stoppin' kisses."

He couldn't help but tease, "So you enjoyed my kisses."

"Aye, I'll not deny it."

He admired her honesty. "If I promise to behave, will you honor me with your company for the next three evenings? We don't even have to dance, Emma. We could do whatever pleases you. All I wish for is you grant me the pleasure of your company."

Her eyes shuttered, and she pulled her full bottom lip between her teeth before she lifted her gaze back to his. "Anythin' I want, huh?"

"Aye." He'd willing agree to anything for an opportunity to be alone with this mesmerizing woman.

The mouth he so desired curved into a wicked grin. "Do ye know how to sew?"

"No."

"But ye do know how to sketch." She tilted her head and narrowed her eyes. "Aye. Ye can meet me at me shop."

He was skeptical about what she had in mind for him, but he didn't care. Closing the space between them, he shifted closer. Her breath hitched, and he stilled.

Gaze locked on his, she leaned forward and asked, "Are ye going to kiss me again to seal our bargain?"

"Would you like that?"

The woman didn't even blink before she responded. "Aye."

Christopher leaned in and kissed her softly. He limited himself to the pressure of her lips, not daring to seek out the taste of her. She tempted him like no other. He was a gentleman, and she was an innocent.

Reluctant for her to leave, he asked, "Will you stay and eat?"

"Nay. I best be off. I've got ladies comin' fer fittin' all day." She stood and bent and gave him a sweet kiss on the cheek and said, "Goodbye fer now."

She left and took a little piece of him with her. It was an odd sensation that he'd never experienced, and he wasn't entirely certain if he cared for the hollow, empty feeling.

CHAPTER TEN

Smoothing out the mint-green silk, Emma sighed. Her last appointment for the day was late. She glanced back down at the shimmering material. The shade of green would highlight its owner's eyes. Lady Arabelle had dared Emma to design a dress for Bronwyn's ball that would tempt a man of the cloth. It was a brash, reckless challenge, and one no sensible modiste would accept, but Emma had been itching to test her skills. Lady Arabelle's youthful form would complement even the most basic of designs, but she wanted a gown that would accentuate her pert bosom and emphasize her petite waist, all in an effort to make the man of her heart submit to his own desires. A tiny spark of guilt pricked Emma's conscience on behalf of the target of Lady Arabelle's scheme. Why the man refused to come up to snuff and offer for the woman boggled Emma's mind. Lady Arabelle was intelligent, well versed in politics, and had a head for investments. It was no wonder

Christopher had once been interested in pursuing her. Lady Arabelle would have made a fine wife for Christopher. Wife. Christopher was on the hunt for a wife.

Emma gripped the edge of the cutting table, short of breath. She inhaled slowly until the stabbing sensations in her chest abated. He should be seeking out a woman more like Lady Arabelle, not negotiating agreements to spend time with the likes of her. She would never manage to be refined and poised like Bronwyn had. Ladies didn't agree to secret meetings alone with a gentleman. And they certainly didn't seek out kisses to seal bargains that were dangerous to their hearts. Never before had a man's perusal caused her body to respond. Instead of revulsion at what Emma believed to be vile male thoughts, Christopher's gaze sparked a sinful curiosity within her. The man's intense stares made her insides quiver, even more than his fiery kisses.

The bell over her shop door tinkled, announcing Lady Arabelle's arrival. The persistant younger lady had made it a weekly habit to visit for an hour or two. More often than not, Lady Arabelle would simply chatter on about the latest *on dit* while Emma sewed or took inventory. At first, Emma hadn't the heart to turn the lady away, believing Lady Arabelle was lonely. However, she wasn't without friends amongst her set, as Emma came to hear all about them. After Lady Arabelle's third visit, the woman confessed she wished to strengthen their family bond. Emma was well aware of Arabelle's tenacity, and if Emma had denied her, Arabelle would simply have devised another scheme. And so each week, Emma waited for Lady Arabelle to burst through her door—for the woman was a whirlwind of energy.

"Emma!" The girl's sweet voice was lyrical even when shouting.

Pulling back the curtain to the back room, Emma smiled and said, "Lady Arabelle, ye finally arrived."

"I apologize. I had a devil of a time escaping. Sebastian and his lectures." Lady Arabelle embraced Emma in a hug. "We heard you will be attending the Hadfield ball. Sebastian would love for you to arrive with us in the Hereford carriage."

How amusing that the news of the coming and goings of a mere dressmaker made it to the ears of the members of the ton. "That's nice of yer brother to offer, but I'm not attending."

"But we were told..." Lady Arabelle released Emma and demanded, "Why not?"

"For me own reasons." Emma swiveled and rounded the table to grab a bowl full of pins. If the woman continued to press, Emma wondered how many pinpricks the woman would endure before she desisted.

Lady Arabelle said, "But Countess Hadfield is your oldest and dearest friend."

Deciding it best not to draw blood, Emma placed the pins next to the mint-green gown that remained laid out on the cutting table.

Emma stomped out of the back room, leaving her client behind. "Bronwyn needs to make new friends."

Coming to a halt next to the measuring table, Emma grabbed a bolt of pink floral satin and let it fall upon the bench with a loud thump, punctuating her statement. It was one thing for a lady to associate herself with a dressmaker but an utter disgrace to claim a bastard as her friend. Emma did not want to embroil Bronwyn in a scandal that was neither of their doing. No. It was best she didn't attend.

Lady Arabelle pressed on. "You can't mean that."

The entreaty chipped a piece of Emma's heart away. Of course she didn't want to lose her best friend. But Emma would rather poke her eye with a needle than to bring shame upon Bronwyn. Why didn't the lady and her brother understand that insisting on claiming her as family would cause tongues to wag, and none of the gossip would be kind or beneficial to their status amongst their peers? Heavens above—Lord Hereford was privy council to the King and Prince Regent. What was he thinking, offering to escort her to the ball?

Emma glared at Lady Arabelle. It was like staring into a looking glass—they shared the same honey-blonde hair, heart-shaped face, and unfashionably lush lips. Bronwyn's guests would have to be blind not to see the family resemblance. Attending the Hadfield ball was out of the question. The Herefords already attracted enough attention. Between Sebastian—unwed, titled and blessed with his papa's handsome features—and Arabelle's beauty and skill at the pianoforte, the family garnered more than its fair share of attention from the matchmaking mamas and patriarchs of the ton.

Emma pushed the bolt of material until it reached the end of the yardstick. Grabbing her shears, she asked,

"Have ye known me to ever lie?" Emma sliced through the material and snapped them closed.

Arabelle jumped. "No. But..."

Stuffing the shears through a loop on her apron, Emma grabbed the satin material she'd cut and made her way over to the closet where the gown she had been designing for herself was housed.

Pushing Emma aside, Arabelle gushed, "Oh my! This gown is glorious." Holding up the ruby red dress to her petite body, Arabelle twirled in a circle.

Emma reached around Arabelle to place a swath of the pink material just below the bustline. "No. This will not work." She discarded the satin and retrieved a wide roll of lace. Holding the fragile lace up to the dress, Emma said, "This gown is not for ye." Although Emma was older, their body shape was yet another similarity they shared. Lady Arabelle could easily fit into the gorgeous gown Emma had envisioned wearing to the ball.

Moving the bolt of material out of the way, Emma asked, "Ye're not really attempting to debauch a man of the cloth—are ye?"

Lady Arabelle laughed. "Of course not. But the man I hope to tempt is as devout in his beliefs as any priest."

"Who is this man?"

"I'm afraid to speak his name. For if Sebastian were ever to find out, he may never let me out of his sight."

Emma snorted. Lady Arabelle wasn't afraid of her brother in the least. "Why? Yer brother is a fair sort."

"Because the man is labeled a notorious rake...and has been for over a decade."

Emma stood in front of Lady Arabelle and removed the dress from the woman's hands. Christopher held the reputation of a rake amongst the Network.

"Lady Arabelle, ye wouldn't be speaking of Mr. Neale, would ye?"

"Emma, you are my aunt, for goodness sake. You should be addressing me as Arabelle at the very least."

A burst of fury rolled through Emma. The woman had avoided her question and had again brought up their familial connection that boiled Emma's blood. "Lady Arabelle, we might be related by blood, but I'm not yer family. I've told ye and yer brother countless times I'll not be claimed as such and have asked ye to stop bouting about such things."

Lady Arabelle crossed her arms and huffed. "We are family. The obstinance that runs through your veins is the same that flows through mine. And to answer your question, while Mr. Neale is devilishly handsome, no. My heart belongs to another man."

Her anger evaporated at Lady Arabelle's answer. "Who?" Emma demanded as she placed the dress and lace upon the table.

"You'll think me a ninny if I tell you his name. But his reputation is without merit." Lady Arabelle was born with a wise old soul. It wasn't surprising she fell in love with an older man. While Emma would never publicly admit it, Lady Arabelle was kin, and Emma wouldn't let any man hurt her family.

Emma said, "Tell me more about this fella of yers."

Arabelle flopped onto the settee and draped her arm

over her face. "He claims he's too debauched for me—that he isn't worthy of my love." With an exaggerated sigh, she continued, "He claims he is past his prime and has resolved to spend the rest of his days as a bachelor."

If Lady Arabelle's behavior was the result of falling in love, then Emma wanted nothing to do with the condition.

"He's right. Yer too good for him. Why don't ye attempt to seduce another man? A man more worthy of ye."

Bolting to sit up straight, Arabelle said, "There is no other for me."

Lor. Unrequited love apparently caused a woman to lose her wits. "Don't be silly. Doesn't Sebastian know of some respectable young lord you could marry?"

"Oh, my brother has a long list of eligible men, but Lord Mar..." Lady Arabelle shook her head and sighed. She rolled back to rest her head upon the arm of the settee and said, "The lord with whom I'm in love with is not on the list."

Blast. If Lady Arabelle had revealed her beau's name, Emma could have had the Network investigate the man. If he proved worthy, she would have devised a scheme to assist the woman in despair lying in the midst of her shop. Her niece. Damnation, it was dangerous to begin thinking of the woman as anything but Lady Arabelle.

Emma looked down at the row of lace she had pinned without thought as they had chatted. She'd designed the gown with Christopher in mind. She shouldn't bring up Christopher, but curiosity won out. "Is Mr. Neale on yer brother's list?" Emma's gut flipped as the word escaped her mouth.

Arabelle raised her head and answered, "Aye." Flinging her arm over her eyes once more, Arabelle continued, "Christopher and I could have lived a life together amicably."

Emma's heart cinched at Arabelle's use of Christopher's given name. It shouldn't bother her. He had courted Arabelle for a spell, after all.

Arabelle sighed. "But have you ever been in a man's presence, and the rest of the world fades away?"

"Aye." Every time Christopher was near. Emma was struck with sadness, realizing she wasn't the only one who fell under Christopher's spell.

"Well, the world still exists when I stand next to Christopher. He is not the one for me." She lifted her arm slightly and peered at Emma. "Wait. How do you know about Christopher and me? We were extremely careful."

"He told me."

Arabelle rolled to her feet and confronted Emma. "Christopher told you. When?"

"Recently." Avoiding Arabelle's searching gaze, Emma busied herself holding various buttons up to the gown.

Wandering about the room, Arabelle said, "Then you already knew I've no interest in Mr. Neale." Arabelle had reverted to referring to him with propriety. What was the chit up to? The mischievous gleam was back in her eyes.

"I thought he perhaps misunderstood your feelings."

"Ha!" Emma jumped at Arabelle's voice right behind

her. "The Mr. Neale I'm acquainted with is extremely insightful and an excellent judge of character. Also, he was never one to talk in riddles, always straight to the point and honest." She tapped Emma on the shoulder. Emma spun around to stare into Arabelle's serious features. "I do care enough for Mr. Neale to be one hundred percent honest with him. He is a wonderful man, and I consider him a dear friend."

A wave of irrational anger on Christopher's behalf at Arabelle's rejection rolled through Emma.

The bell over the door tinkled, and Emma's dad appeared.

Tipping his hat, he nodded. "Lady Arabelle." He glanced about the shop before shutting the door behind him.

Grabbing her reticule from the settee, Arabelle headed for the door. "Mr. Lennox, it is a pleasure to see you, but your appearance means the hour grows late, and it's time for me to return home." Arabelle straightened from her perfect little curtsy.

Emma called out, "I'll expect ye next week for a fittin'."

"Splendid. I'm looking forward to seeing your newest creation." Arabelle winked and turned to leave.

Mr. Lennox opened the door and said, "Let me escort you to your carriage—it's already dark outside."

Emma stood by the front door as her dad gallantly walked Arabelle to the waiting vehicle. Once her niece was safely tucked inside, her dad marched back and said, "Ye shouldn't be allowin' her to stay so late."

"She's hard to get rid of."

"I heard ye are expectin' another visitor this eve."

The Network's gossip mill was hard to evade. "Yes, I'm expectin' Mr. Neale to arrive later."

"But ye've decided not to attend Bronwyn's bloody ball. For wot good reason is he payin' ye a visit?"

"He's offered to help...."

"Help ye with wot? Pinning gowns?" her dad teased and then his lips thinned into a straight line. "I don't trust him. I want to know his intentions." He took a step closer and stared down at her. "Ye're me daughter, and I'll not have anyone take advantage of yer kind heart."

"What if it is I who takes advantage of him?"

"Yer mum didn't want me to share me thoughts on the matter, but men are highly motivated to say and do anythin' to win a pretty girl's affection. Yer mum believes Mr. Neale is an honorable one, jus' like his brother. And if he's taken an interest in ye, well, ye best be thinkin' wot to say if he asks ye to marry him."

"Marry Mr. Neale? I've only jus' met him."

"Lord Hadfield's dictate for his brother to marry by season's end is well known. We all know of Lady Arabelle's rejection of Mr. Neale's pursuit and his sudden interest in ye. Yer mum asks ye to consider the matter carefully."

"He's not interested in marriage to me."

"How do ye know?"

"If Mr. Neale did propose, it would be out of convenience. Rejected by a lady, he is in desperate need of a woman to marry. I'll not marry a man who's not in love with me, as you are in love with me mum."

"Girl, come here." He sat and waited for her to sit next to him. "Do ye know how long it took me to ask yer mum for her hand?"

"I'm guessin' not long. The two of ye are always fawnin' over each other."

"Wrong. I've loved yer mum pretty much from the day we met, but it took me three long years for me ask her to marry me. And then there was the matter of the Council. Do ye know why it took me three years?"

"Nay."

"I didn't believe I was good enough to be the husband to a Network Council member. Yer grandma hit me over the head and told me wot I want ye to hear—live life and love without fear."

"But Mr. Neale will become an official PORF upon marryin', and his wife too will become a PORF. I'm not..."

"Girl, ye'd make a fine PORF. Ye have good instincts, and ye're born to do great things. Look at wot ye have already made of yerself." He gave her a hug, kissed the top of her head. "I'm proud of ye, and yer mum and me, we support ye whatever ye decide." With one last squeeze, her dad turned and left.

Mute, Emma followed behind her dad and slowly turned the locks one by one. His footsteps faded, but she remained rooted next to the door. A few days ago, she had pondered over her future—secretly wishing for more. Then she met Christopher, and her life suddenly became more complicated yet exhilarating. Aside from enjoying and longing for more of the man's heart-stopping kisses, Emma was drawn to the complex gentleman who was nothing like the man the Network reports had portrayed. Flattered that Christopher wanted to spend more time together, she hadn't pressed him to share his reasons. She herself couldn't precisely explain why she felt compelled to seek out his company and felt adrift when they were apart. Nevertheless, she would have to find out Christopher's true intentions tonight before matters became more convoluted.

CHAPTER ELEVEN

*N*odding to the two young burly men assigned to watch over Emma's shop, Christopher noted their unusual frosty nature towards him. He hadn't managed to ascertain their names, but he knew they were among a rotation of six men who always saw to Emma's safety. Whispers amongst the Network staff he employed clearly indicated Emma was a highly respected member —the eldest child to a Network elder. The Network apparently cared little about her paternal bloodline, only that she was as fierce a leader as his sister-in-law, Bronwyn. It was no wonder the pair were fast friends. In fact, the blue blood that ran through Emma's veins was considered her single flaw. Her destiny to hold a seat upon the Network Elders' Council explained the extra protection Emma received, for which he was grateful. The dangers of Emma living all alone gave him heart palpitations, and after her morning visit, he couldn't banish the idea of having her safe and living under his roof.

Christopher approached the front door, and just before he rapped on the glass, he turned back and scanned the area. The guards were closer than usual. Best to set them at ease. He walked back to face the cold stares of the young men. "I'm not a threat to her."

The older looking of the two stuck out his chin and said, "What business do ye have callin' this late at night?"

Apparently, it *was* possible to keep some secrets safe from the Network. He'd claimed he simply wished to spend more time with the woman, but it was a lie. He wanted to see her seated at his table, every meal, morn, noon, and eve. He craved her kisses. He needed Emma. But he was no fool. The woman didn't trust easy, and even though she'd eagerly participated in their embraces, he would have to prove his worth to her before she would even consider the idea of having him.

The younger man chimed in, "Ye're not marked. Our loyalty belongs to Emma, so ye best have a good reason to be visitin'."

"Are you questioning my intentions?"

"Aye." The pair replied in unison.

"Emma is perfectly safe with me." He was a gentleman, for goodness sake. What was in his blasted Network file to give Emma's guards pause? He had been a damned saint for the past two years, with little time for anything but work.

Ignoring the wary looks on the guards' faces, Christopher swiveled to march back up to the shop's front door. Guilt at not having been the model gentleman during their previous encounters resulted in his fist striking against the glass harder than he intended.

"Stop yer bloody poundin' or ye'll break me bleedin' door." Emma peeked from behind the curtain. Her eyes widened and lit with excitement. With each click of a latch being released, a muscle in his body relaxed.

The door swung open, and Emma invited him in. Christopher stood next to her admiring her swift moves securing the door once more. Yes, this woman was the woman he wanted. A chuckle escaped him as he recalled Bronwyn's request to assist Emma with her speech. He was loath to disappoint his sister-in-law, but he'd not be attempting to change the woman standing beside him— she was magnificent in her own right.

She beamed a smile up at him. "Wot's so amusing?"

"Nothing. I'm simply happy to be here."

"I'm glad ye are here too." Emma reached for his hand. "I've got lots of plans for ye." She led him over to the settee on the shop floor.

Removing his hat, gloves, and coat, he asked, "Oh, really? Would you care to share what you have in store for me?"

The minx pursed her lips, scattering every gentle-manly thought he possessed. She removed the items from his hands and placed them in a neat pile upon the piece of furniture. His mind was busy imagining them lying upon it—naked.

"Ye did agree to do wotever I wanted." She rested her hands flat against his chest.

Had she felt his heart jump through his waistcoat?

The mischievous slant of her lips and the twinkle of desire in her eyes had him lowering his head to her ear. "Was there something specific you wanted from me now?"

Emma boldly slid her arms about his neck and brought his mouth to hers. Giving in to temptation, his tongue slid over her lower lip, prompting her to open for him. But Emma took charge, and it was he who was lost.

Only when she broke the kiss for air did he regain his mental facilities. Plump pink lips beckoned for his attention, but her guards' questions had him pulling back. Instead, he said, "I've been thinking about you all day."

"Have ye?"

"Aye, but I've been warned to behave myself."

"By whom?"

"Well, earlier, my dear older brother came by and paid me a visit. Quizzed me as to the purpose of our meetings now that you had no intention of attending Bronwyn's ball. My rather vague answers appeased neither him nor the ears beyond the walls and doors of my office."

Emma placed what would otherwise be a chaste kiss upon his cheek, but at that moment, it sent a bolt of pure desire down to his loins. "It's yer own fault. If ye weren't a known rake, then all would be well."

He pulled back but didn't fully release her. "Rake? I've been chaste as a monk for the past two years!" Who was filling her pretty head with such notions? He swallowed a groan. His behavior had been far from innocent.

"Really? Hmm..." She cocked her head to one side. A patch of creamy skin on her neck beckoned him.

He didn't hesitate. He circled the soft, delicate skin with his tongue and then pressed his lips to the spot. "Aye, no one tempts me like you do."

A soft moan from the back of her throat had him suckling the tender skin. If he didn't stop, he would leave a mark. Straightening, he gazed down at Emma. She lowered her arms and reached behind her back for his hand once more. Reluctantly, he released his hold about her waist and threaded his fingers with hers. Her eyes darted to the stairs that led up to her private lodging. It was an invitation that he was sorely tempted to accept. But he wanted more than just her body. Lowering them both to the settee, Christopher said, "Tell me, what plans did you have for us this eve?"

"Me plans?" Emma shook her head. A flare of desire flashed in her eyes but was quickly blanketed as she shifted away. He didn't like the additional inch of space she had placed between them, but it was probably for the best. It would ensure he avoided the temptation to divest her of her dress and make his earlier imaginings become a reality. While waiting for her to speak, he attempted to clear his mind by reciting the Latin alphabet.

Emma ran her palms over her thighs before meeting his gaze. "Me dad paid me a visit earlier."

"As he does every eve, does he not?"

"Aye." Emma lowered her eyes to her tightly clasped hands. "Why did ye push to spend more time with me?"

"Why did you agree if you didn't wish the same?"

She shrugged. Emma wouldn't meet his gaze.

His stomach clenched at the sickening thought that she had agreed out of obligation and duty and not out of a desire for his company. He reached out to lift her chin until their eyes met. "Please tell me you didn't consent to our meetings because you took an oath to serve PORFs."

He couldn't read her thoughts behind her shuttered eyes. Gone was the woman seeking out his kisses, replaced by a woman he didn't recognize. Had all their interactions been merely her sense of duty to see to his needs? He waited, wanting her to deny it. Hoping she'd tell him she was as spellbound as he was. Wishing her days had been filled with thoughts of him as his days were with her.

Emma remained silent.

Christopher released a sigh of resignation. Emma wasn't interested in his company. She didn't care for him the same way he'd come to cherish her.

"I release you from our agreement." He donned his coat, hat, and gloves. Speaking to the top of her bent head, he continued, "I won't subject you to any more lessons or attempt to further court you." Christopher trudged to the door and let himself out. With the door ajar facing the empty street, he said, "I shan't forget you, Emma Lennox, but I'll not bother you anymore."

SITTING on the floor in the middle of her store, Emma finished hemming Lady Arabelle's gown. The tears that had blurred her vision finally rolled down her cheek as she tied a knot and cut the thread away from the gown. Recalling the events of Christopher's visit was torture. None of it made sense. First, he had arrived early, catching her off guard. Armed with only a half-concocted scheme to determine Christopher's true intentions, Emma had relied upon her instincts. Caught up in his charming spell, she sought out his kisses. Knowing Christopher was a gentleman and wouldn't take her innocence unless he intended to marry her, she had dared to invite him up to her bed. Her pride was punctured when he rejected her offer, choosing to remain on the shop floor.

Not one for games, Emma changed tactics and blurted the question she needed to be answered. Except she forgot she was dealing with a barrister who skillfully countered her inquires with questions of his own. Questions she wasn't ready to answer. She should have answered him. She should have told him the truth—she hadn't agreed to meet with him out of a sense of duty. Confessed that he had transformed her routine days into adventures. Admitted when he was near, she dared to wish for more.

But when he had uttered the word courtship, she thought her hearing faulty. A series of images had flashed before her. Christopher standing before Reverend Rivers at her church. The PORF mark upon her ankle. Her parents waving from afar. All leaving her mute as Christopher left her shop.

Emma wiped the tears away from the edge of her jaw

with the back of her hand. Rolling to her feet, she walked over to the far wall. She ran her hand over the cabinets and drawers designed and crafted by her dad. Her parents' support had never once wavered in all the years she'd pursued her dreams. Wandering through the bolts of material, ribbon, and lace, Emma mumbled, "Could I really give all this up for a life with Christopher?"

Argh. Bronwyn had once accused Emma of having a terrible habit of taking actions that prevented her from gaining what she most desired. Is that what she had done this eve?

Halfway up the steps to her sanctuary, she turned back to scan the shop floor once more. And for the first time ever, instead of pride flowing through her veins, a cloak of emptiness enveloped about her. Her gaze landed on the settee that she and Christopher had occupied earlier. Tears welled and spilled onto her cheeks. Should she risk the life she had built for herself for an uncertain future?

A future that had the potential to force her to emerge from the shadows of the Network and be thrust into his world alongside the ton, which she had carefully avoided for most of her youth. Until the fateful day she decided to offer her services to the secretive Lady Lucy, the first female Agent of the Home Office. Lady Lucy had been young and in need of the Network's help. Emma felt a kinship for the woman she couldn't ignore. Similarly, Emma couldn't deny the young, grieving Lord Hereford an audience when he appeared on her doorstep, extending her the same offer his papa had years before—

for Emma to live under the protection of the Hereford title. She had declined the offer of residence and the generous dowry bequeathed to her. Instead, she extracted a promise from Lord Hereford to never reveal her inheritance and requested the funds be donated to an orphanage run by the Network. Like her mum, she had declined all of Lord Hereford and his papa's attempts to atone for the trespasses of the past and would continue to do so.

With a heavy heart, she placed a hand on the railing and mounted each step, ready to rest her weary head. Feet firmly planted on the landing, her eyes watered again gazing at the space she had experienced her first real kiss...with Christopher. Emma clutched her stomach. Not even a day had passed, and already she missed him. Crossing the empty space, Emma shuffled behind the screen and crawled into bed. Thankful no one was about, she buried her face in her pillow and wept.

CHAPTER TWELVE

*T*he ink bled into the paper as the nib of Christopher's quill stilled. Landon's thunderous booted footsteps echoed through the hall. Damnation, he was in no mood to deal with the Earl of Hadfield or the Head PORF, or whatever role his brother was fulfilling today. Long gone were the days where their brotherly talks consisted of which clients they should accept and who was to dine with their lonely mama. The only positive to come of Landon inheriting the Hadfield title was their mama's reentrance to society and her reunion with friends of old. Their mama's days were again filled with activity. Aside from conducting subtle inquires for either Theo or Landon, their mama was busy planning for the arrival of the newest member of the Neale family that Bronwyn carried. A vision of Emma round with child flashed before him. He dropped the quill to rub his temples. The glimpses into his future were rare occurrences past his eighteenth birthday, but he had learned not to ignore them. How could this be—Emma wasn't interested in his pursuit.

The heavy footsteps came to a stop at his door. Expecting Landon to barge his way in, Christopher scanned his desk. Damnation. He crumpled the ruined case summary and skillfully launched it at the bin by the door before gathering the incomplete drawings of Emma. Sketches that had distracted him from his ever-growing pile of work. He stuffed them beneath a stack of files mere moments before the door swung open.

Focused upon the case file before him, Christopher barked, "I'm busy."

"For the past three days, I hear. Apart from returning to your residence to change, you've been holed up here."

His brother's tone bristled Christopher's ire. He didn't need Landon meddling in his affairs. "Don't you ever tire of hearing reports on how others are living their lives?"

Not bothering to remove his coat, Landon sat in the chair opposite him. "No one's seen you eat or sleep."

Mayhap his brother intended for this to be one of his quicker visits. Landon placed his hat and gloves upon the table and leisurely crossed his legs. Damnation! Landon clearly had no intention of leaving any time soon.

"Well, as you can see, I'm still breathing." Christopher clenched his jaw. After his disastrous evening with Emma, even the act of filling his lungs was a task. He'd never experienced such acute pain in his chest as he had leaving Emma's store. He had no desire to ever endure such agony again. Yet the flashes of his future continued to feature Emma.

"Then who died?"

Not who but *what* had died within him. Hope. Desire. Dreams of a different future. Love. The hollow feeling inside him wasn't due to the death of any one of those things, but perhaps all of them.

Landon unfolded and leaned forward. "Brother?"

He blinked, and his brother came into focus. "Beg pardon?"

"You only ever skip a meal when someone you know has passed. So who was it? Must have been someone you deeply cared for you to forgo food for three days." Landon's gaze, filled with concern, tracked his movements as Christopher rested his elbows upon the desk and rubbed his aching temples.

Christopher sighed. "No one has died." He was exhausted, and there was no point in continuing the conversation that would merely result in more hours of brooding over Emma.

"Then what is the matter?"

This wasn't something his big brother could assist him with, and telling Landon as much would only agitate the man more. "Nothing. Don't you have more pressing duties than harp on about my eating habits?"

Straightening and crossing his arms in front of his chest, Landon said, "Mama threatened to come down here and feed you like a babe if I didn't resolve whatever it was that was causing your lack of self-care. Shall I inform her to proceed with her visit?"

The shiver that ran down his spine was fierce. Christopher wouldn't put it past his mama to do such a ghastly thing. "It's a woman."

"It always is. Who is this woman?" Landon drummed his fingers against his upper arm. "I'm not leaving until I have a name."

It wasn't a threat, it was a statement, and Landon was never easily dissuaded.

"Emma."

"My wife's best friend. The woman you claimed was merely a friend." Landon's voice deepened to a bone-chilling tone. "A woman who is a key Network member under my protection."

"Yes. Emma Lennox."

A lesser man might have flinched at his brother's stern bark. "What happened?"

Christopher raised his head and snapped, "Nothing happened. That's the problem. Emma wants naught to do with me." He had been fooled by the woman's responsive kisses. His plan to court her out of the sight of prying eyes and meddling members of family and Network had failed. But under his big brother's disconcerting gaze, he finally admitted to the heart of the matter. "All I want is to be in the same room as her."

"Interesting. A woman who isn't tempted by your handsome features or your charm and wit." The corner of Landon's mouth quirked up, revealing his blasted dimple. "Hmm...I don't believe it. Emma is a fine judge of character. Are you sure she doesn't return your regard?"

"How can one mistake silence? She didn't deny that

the only reason she agreed to see me was because of her blasted oath."

Landon's features relaxed and his eyes softened with what Christopher guessed was sympathy. "Why did you arrange the meetings with Emma?"

"Obviously to court her."

"Why? As a means to obtain the mark?"

Christopher stared at his brother. Granted, they hadn't been in each other's company much these past two years, but Landon couldn't seriously believe he would consider marrying someone he didn't care for. Love. He stood and meandered over to the window. Since Landon brought up the topic of the mark, Christopher asked, "Do you not think me worthy to receive the mark?"

"What a preposterous statement. Of course, you are worthy. It's just that once you receive it, your life will be forever changed."

"No. Our lives were altered the day our cousin Baldwin died." Christopher peered out the window. Men assigned to Landon's protection patrolled the perimeter. He turned back to find Landon pacing. Christopher waited until his brother turned toward him before saying, "Do you ever wish..."

"Yes, every damn day. I wish he had survived and inherited the title and the role of Head PORF. With every decision or order I make, I instantly question what Baldwin would have done. Would our cousin have retained and claimed the blasted rondure that made me head of this whole mess, or would he have managed somehow to bury it and hide it from all once again?"

The material of Landon's greatcoat fell to the side as he placed a fisted hand upon his hip, revealing the bandage about his ribs.

Striding to come face-to-face with his brother, Christopher grabbed Landon by the shoulders. "Good lord, what happened to you?"

Landon shrugged him off and resumed pacing. His brother was never one to stay still. It was why he was more suited to the courtroom than sitting in mediation. "Nothing to fuss over. I merely had a coughing spell. The doctor believes I might have fractured a rib or two."

Damn his brother's lung condition. But it wouldn't do to harp on it. Landon already harbored enough fear of an early demise. Christopher asked, "Are you trying to send our mama to an early grave?"

"I could ask the same of you. You have her extremely worried. Whereas she has no clue about my injury."

Urgh. Landon hadn't lost his abilities as a barrister, swiftly turning the focus of the conversation back to him. Christopher smiled and said, "Ah, but it won't be long before Mama finds out. She *always* does."

They both chuckled, but Landon winced as they shared the moment of levity.

"You know, without an heir, should something happen to you, I will inherit the title but not the rondure as long as I remain unmarked."

Landon arched a brow and said, "If you wish to receive the mark, then marry."

"Dammit, Landon. As a Neale, it is my familial right to serve the Crown as you do." Christopher ran a hand through his hair and rested it on the back of his neck. "Who would you have me marry?"

"Brother, you have had women at your beck and call since...well, since you hit puberty. Honestly, when I made the blasted proclamation, I seriously hadn't considered it would take you this long to find love." Landon ceased his pacing. "We digress. What needs to be done for you to resume your normal, carefree disposition everyone is so fond of?"

"There is naught for *you* to do." Christopher didn't want his brother involved. "Promise not to share a word about Emma to *any* of the Hadfield women." He wanted Emma to come to him willingly, not out of duty.

"You know I can't make that promise." Landon grabbed his hat and gloves. "But I have faith you shall have matters in hand soon enough. As always, I'm at your disposal should you find yourself in need of assistance."

"Speaking of assistance, I've hired Weathersbee to be my secretary."

Tugging on his gloves, Landon asked, "You can't be referring to Lord Weathersbee? The man is nearly old enough to be our father."

"I am. The man is not quite that old. He's five years younger than Mama. His lordship humbly stated in his application that despite his middling years, his mind was sharp, and it was time he utilized his Oxford education." In fact, it had been Weathersbee's maturity that had swayed Christopher to hire him.

"Weathersbee. Third son of a Marquess. A fair businessman. Wealthy in his own right. Hmm. Begs the question—why would he seek employment?"

"I've no idea as to what prompted his interest in the position. However, he has the education and the maturity I'm seeking, and so I hired him." Once marked, Christopher's duties and priorities would change. The protection of the Crown would be his priority. He needed a man he could trust to assist with the running of the offices should Christopher find himself off on a mission.

Landon remained rooted next to the door, a pensive look upon his face.

Christopher said, "Not everyone has nefarious intentions."

"Mayhap, but nonetheless, I shall be making inquiries. My thanks—Bronwyn will be relieved to know you have found her replacement."

"No one can replace my dear sister-in-law, but I shall settle for Weathersbee."

At the mention of his wife, Landon's eyes lit up. His brother left without another word, no doubt to hunt down Bronwyn.

Returning to his desk, Christopher sat down and pulled out a clean sheet of parchment. Intending to draft a proposal Emma might consider, he picked up his quill. Bold, independent Emma. He searched for the words to express the intangible pull he felt towards her, but his vast legal vocabulary fell short. Instead, all that came to mind were two words: Marry me. But Emma deserved a proper courtship or at least one explicitly designed with her preferences in mind. Emma's aversion to the ton ruled out an invitation for a carriage ride in Hyde Park or an evening at the theater. He needed more information on the woman. It would be a challenge, but if he was to become a Hadfield PORF, responsible for investigating and gathering intel, this would be excellent practice.

CHAPTER THIRTEEN

*E*mma refrained from rolling her eyes as Lord
Hereford paced in front of her. The furniture
in the Hereford townhouse appeared inviting, but the
oversized winged back chair that dwarfed Emma was far
from comfortable. The cushion was firm and hardly
worn, as if no one had ever sat in the bloomin' thing
before. In fact, none of the pieces were aged with wear.
Perhaps Lady Arabelle did not care to entertain, or this
drawing room was reserved for her brother's interroga-
tions. After all, the man was a former Foreign Office
agent.

Emma's stomach rumbled, having skipped the
nooning meal. "Why 'ave ye summoned me?"

Lord Hereford stopped, looked at her, and then shook
his head.

He repeated the action two more times before Emma
sighed and stood ready to leave if the man couldn't
summon the gumption to speak his mind. "I've got me a

mountain of sewing to do, me lord, so unless ye care to explain the dire emergency ye claimed to be experiencin' in yer note, I'll jus' be on me way."

He stopped and turned to face Emma. His eyes filled with worry, and another emotion Emma had never seen before. Fear. No. Pride. No. She couldn't place it, but whatever had caused him to send a carriage to her shop to fetch her was indeed a matter of import.

Clearing his throat, Lord Hereford finally found his voice. "I wish to ask you to refrain from assisting my sister in her devilish schemes."

Ah. Arabelle. Emma should have known the lady was the center of her brother's concerns. Orphaned an early age, with only the servants left to raise them, the siblings were extremely close.

The man was being run ragged by his sister. Emma took pity on Lord Hereford and got straight to the point. "Are ye talkin' about the dress she requested for Lady Hadfield's ball?"

"Yes, I am. I bloody well had to sequester my dear sister's maid for an hour before the chit finally confessed. God only knows what the staff was thinking with me having the girl in here all that time."

Confirmation Emma had guessed correctly at the purpose of the room had her grinning. But the distress in Lord Hereford's last sentence quickly prompted a quick response. "Ye are nothin' like yer grandfather, and yer staff knows it."

Wrinkles about the man's eyes appeared, aging him beyond his eight and twenty years. Hands clenched firmly behind his back, he said, "Sounds absurd, but knowing his blood runs through my veins, I'm ever vigilant against developing his wicked ways."

Lord Hereford's statement struck her heart. Hearing that they shared the same fear placed a large hole in the wall she had built to keep her distance from Lord Hereford—Sebastian. Fustian. Both Hereford siblings were whittling away her resistance to their company.

Guilt at having agreed to design a dress for devilish intentions shot through Emma. Back straight, she said, "Yer sister is stubborn. No changin' her mind once she has a plan. Best be involved rather than not know."

"If you won't desist, then I shall have to cease paying her modiste bill."

Sebastian's reply was quick and decisive. Lord Hadfield had chosen wisely in installing Sebastian as privy council to the King and Prinny. At the time of his appointment, Emma had her doubts, but there was no denying the man pacing in front of her was intelligent and possessed great honor. Emma waited for Sebastian to complete a circuit about the room. She lifted her chin and said, "I don't charge ye."

Standing with perfect posture, he paused directly before Emma. "Is that so?" He stroked his chin and added, "Arabelle has much to explain. I've been much too lenient with her since my return from the Continent."

Emma laughed and wondered what Arabelle was doing with the extra funds she'd been commandeering from her brother. Meeting Sebastian's eyes, which were so similar to his sister's and her own, Emma felt all her defenses crumble. She'd not be denying Sebastian the connection he and his sister had persisted in forming with her.

Brows knitted together, Sebastian asked, "Do *you* know the identity of this man my sister is intent on marrying?" The flicker of the firelight in his eyes highlighted the man's anxiety.

With a shake of her head, Emma replied, "Don't ye?"

Releasing a defeated sigh, he said, "She won't share the blasted man's name. But I know her too well—Arabelle will not give up."

Emma hazarded it was a trait Sebastian shared. And she herself.

She should stay out of the affair entirely, but curiosity got the better of her. "If ye were to know the gentleman's name, wot would ye do?"

Sebastian cracked his knuckles. "Demand a bloody explanation from the fool."

"'Tis no wonder yer sister refuses to name him. Ye look like ye might kill the fellow. Arabelle is no pea goose."

Turning on his heel, Sebastian returned to pacing about the room. Resigned she wouldn't be leaving anytime soon, Emma slid further back in her chair. She ran her hand over the crewel-embroidered wool fabric. Tracing the blue thread of a daisy brought an image of Bronwyn to mind. Bronwyn had reassured Emma that she accepted the decision not to attend her debut ball, but Bronwyn hadn't managed to mask the disappointment in her voice.

"I need your help." Sebastian's declaration brought Emma's attention back to the man who looked like he had solved the world's problems.

"Fer wot?"

"I know Arabelle has some sordid plan for the Hadfield ball." Waving a finger at her, he said, "You were invited. I need you to attend; help me to ensure Arabelle doesn't embroil herself in some scandal and to ferret out the man's identity."

She had banished the idea of attending. Christopher would be there. It would break her to see him dancing with another after experiencing it herself. No. He needed to find a wife, and she needed... Well, she wasn't sure exactly how to fix the emptiness in her heart that had taken up residence since Christopher departed from her store, but she'd find a way.

She glared at her host. "Ye're a bloomin' former Foreign Agent and the bleedin' advisor to the King and the Prince Regent. Surely ye have access to resources that can assist ye."

Sebastian's eyes narrowed. She imagined it was a look similar to her own.

Placing both hands on his hips, he said, "There is one thing that runs strong in the Hereford bloodlines... well, actually two: obstinacy and the stout ability to prevent anyone but of their choosing to come close. Arabelle trusts you. She might confide in you who the blighter is."

The concern on Lord Hereford's features was heart wrenching. Arabelle was lucky to have an older sibling concerned for her welfare. Sebastian's gaze softened, and he asked again, "Will you assist me?"

Bah. The stubborn set of the man's jaw told her she'd not be leaving until he received her promise to help. Their family did not need to weather a scandal. And Lord Hadfield would be displeased if Sebastian's post were placed in jeopardy. In Emma's heart, she knew even without those motivations, she would do anything to protect her family and the Herefords. *Like it or not, we're family.* "I will help you. But I'll not be attending the bleedin' ball, or at least not in plain sight."

"Grand. Shall I ring for refreshments while we discuss how to oust the man from hiding?"

Returning Sebastian's victorious grin with a smirk of her own, Emma said, "I be thinkin' we need somethin' a bit stronger than tea—wouldn't ye agree?"

Chuckling as he made his way to the sideboard, Sebastian offered, "French brandy?"

"Ye got any Scottish whiskey?"

He turned to face her. "We definitely share a bloodline."

"No need to remind me," Emma mumbled. She rolled to her feet and crossed the plush carpet to stand before the fire. Holding her hands out, Emma soaked up the warmth. The room's atmosphere transformed from intimidating to one she could become accustomed to—with time.

Sebastian handed her a tumbler with a splash of amber liquid. She needed more than the half-finger offered, but she accepted the glass and rolled it between her palms. Faced with the prospect of becoming a frequent visitor of the Hereford residence, Emma downed the entire contents of her glass. While it no longer sent tendrils of fear down her spine, it also didn't hold any appeal.

Taking the empty tumbler from her hand, Sebastian said, "I did as you requested. I gave the funds bequeathed to you to the orphanage anonymously. However, I will have you know that I've recently had my own final will and testament redrafted. It provides for a small cottage by the sea, unencumbered to the Hereford title of course, and a modest amount of funds to be bestowed upon you, should I come to an untimely demise."

Emma followed her nephew to the sideboard. "Why would ye do such a foolish thing?"

"I assure you, I am no fool." He pulled the stopper from the decanter that housed the tasty malt whiskey that had gone down her gullet with ease. Both glasses received a finger and a half this time. "My lawyer assures me there shall be no gifting to another on your behalf this time."

Bloomin' stubborn Hereford blood. Emma took her tumbler and sipped the whiskey that doubtless cost as much as a gown or two. She didn't want handouts or charity. Peering into the amber liquid, the same color as Christopher's eyes, Emma was struck with an idea. "I shall have to consult me own legal counsel on the matter."

With a nod, Sebastian said, "As you wish." His all too quick agreement gave Emma pause. She replayed the last few moments over in her head. All of it seemed genuine, yet the skin on the back of her neck prickled.

Sebastian placed a hand on her elbow and guided her to the wing-backed chair she had occupied earlier. "Shall we begin discussing our scheme to deal with dear Arabelle?"

Settling back into the seat cushion that had molded to her, Emma replied, "Why do I suspect you already have a plan?"

"Because I do. All I need you to do is—"

Emma emptied her glass. It was going to be a long night of negotiations.

CHAPTER FOURTEEN

*W*eary, Christopher silently trod through the empty building. The idea of breaking his word for the first time ever didn't bode well. He had told Emma he would leave her be, but that wasn't going to be possible. He had to see her. A flicker of a flame seeped beneath the door frame of Bronwyn's office. Landon would have his head if Bronwyn was still at it well past their agreed hours.

Christopher poked his head in. "Weathersbee. What the devil are you doing here?" He entered the office and confronted the older lord, whose spectacles were perched on the tip of his nose.

"Ah. Mr. Neale." Weathersbee rose and gestured to the vacant seat, ignoring Christopher's question.

Damnation, this was his office. His papa's voice boomed—*Always respect your elders.*

As soon as Christopher was seated, the old man continued, "I met with Countess Hadfield this afternoon and believed it would behoove me to stay to review a few summaries."

Christopher peered at the two stacks of files upon the desk. "A few, you say."

Weathersbee removed his spectacles, letting them swing indolently between his forefinger and thumb. "Fascinating that case facts from decades ago are still relevant to current day matters, is it not?"

"Mayhap relevant but not at all practical." Christopher's wish for legal reform meant his papa had encouraged him to focus on the finer points of civil and business law. Christopher's success had seen to it that Neale & Sons was considered the absolute best in drafting the complicated foreign trade agreements that led to many successful joint ventures by investors. Some of which had led to the restocking of the Hadfield coffers.

Folding his eyewear and placing them neatly on top of the short pile, Weathersbee said, "There are some other rather interesting matters the firm assists with. In particular, rather intricate agreements with foreign parties—Americans?"

Weathersbee was clearly no indolent titled gentleman. The old man kept current on world affairs and was extremely astute in reading his opponent's body language.

Christopher considered avoiding the tenuous topic of his aid to Lord Burke. But if Weathersbee was to be in charge of Neale & Sons while he was abroad, Christopher needed to trust the old man. "I assume you are referring to Lord Burke's dealings with Mr. Suttingham.

Americans are notoriously difficult, but to date, I've managed to keep matters in hand."

Weathersbee picked up his spectacles and replaced them upon his nose. "It will be rather difficult to fill the shoes of Countess Hadfield. She is a remarkable woman."

Christopher inwardly sighed, relieved to have avoided discussing in detail Lord Burke's association with the American merchant. Christopher grinned. "Aye. But I believe you are up for the task; otherwise, I'd not have hired you."

The old man chuckled. "I do not wish to give you cause to question your decision, but now that I've paused, I believe it is time I seek out my bed."

Weathersbee rolled his shoulders and arched his back. The old man didn't possess the body of an overindulgent lord. His solid chest and muscled arms bespoke of someone who regularly partook in physical exercise. Like his papa and Landon, before he inherited, Christopher avoided the sporting clubs the lords typically held memberships to. Fencing and bare-fisted sparring were of no interest. Christopher preferred activities that involved more than two participants—cricket had been a favorite pastime at Cambridge. His recent correspondence with the mercenary but wealthy tobacco merchant, Mr. Suttingham, included a rather interesting passage on a game that was fast developing into a favorite pastime across the pond—baseball. Communications from Christopher's ever-increasing number of associates from the New World continually piqued his curiosity. The idea that a man was judged by his character and efforts and not his heritage was alluring. Before Landon inherited, Christopher had seriously contemplated emigrating to the New World. A chance to establish a life for himself out of the shadows of his successful older brother. Those dreams were dashed when the responsibilities of the firm his papa had worked hard to establish fell upon him.

Weathersbee stood next to Christopher, hat, gloves, and coat already donned, ready to leave. "Care to join me for a late supper?"

"That sounds like a grand idea." It would be nice to share a meal with another for a change.

They left the office, and Weathersbee's coach rolled to a stop out front. Before entering the vehicle, Christopher scanned his surroundings and nodded to his Network guards. They were never fond of changes in his routine. Christopher had already determined he was no longer happy with his decision to remain apart from Emma. But first, he'd fortify his nerves with a brandy and a beefsteak from Brooks's.

WEATHERSBEE SPEARED a potato and raised his fork to his mouth. "You seem rather distracted this eve."

"I apologize. My mind is a whirl at present." Christopher had crafted a number of phrases he wished to share with Emma, but none seemed appropriate nor adequate. "My thanks for the invitation to supper." His half-eaten beefsteak no longer held its initial appeal. In fact, his stomach was clenched tight in knots at the prospect of seeing Emma again.

"Perhaps I could assist. After all, I am in your employ to do such."

"The issue is of a personal nature, not one related to Neale & Sons."

The man's brows lowered. "Ah. I see this has to do with a woman. Having never married, I do not claim to have any idea how to deal with the creatures." Weathersbee took another bite of his meal. He took his time chewing and swallowing before he continued, "However, it is my humble opinion that a man should brave rejection and hurt rather than be left to wonder if his regard might have been returned by the woman he loves."

"So, you braved rejection and have remained unmarried."

"No. I was a coward. I feared my lady love's rebuff, and by the time I garnered enough courage to ask for her hand, she'd already chosen another." Weathersbee placed both knife and fork down and grabbed for his glass of brandy. Leaning back in his chair, he added, "Don't dither, Mr. Neale. Go seek the woman you love." He raised his glass to his lips, but over the rim of the glass, the old man's gaze never left Christopher.

He shouldn't pry into the man's private affairs, but the question rolled off Christopher's tongue. "Why did you not marry another?" Damnation. The flash of pain in the old man's eyes was precisely what Christopher wished to avoid.

"There was no other for me." He downed the

remainder of his drink and placed the glass upon the table. The blaze of the fire and the three candles upon the table provided more than sufficient lighting for Christopher to study Weathersbee's features as they transformed from relaxed to tortured to resolved before he said, "Regardless of the number of days, months, or years that have passed, there hasn't been another woman's image who invades my thoughts day and night."

Blast it all. From the moment she blazed right past him on his brother's front steps, there hadn't been a day Christopher hadn't thought of Emma. "I shall heed your advice, Weathersbee. No more dawdling."

"You are a good and honorable man, Mr. Neale. Far more perceptive than I'd given you credit for." The footman had refilled his glass, and Weathersbee rose it in salute. "The woman would be a fool not to return your affection."

Striding out the private dining room of the gentlemen's club, Christopher glanced about at the number of men littered about in chairs, partaking in idle chatter with a drink in their hands. Why did they remain here and not return home to their women? Recognizing a few of the lords as he passed them on his way to the front door, Christopher sighed. These gentlemen had wed out of duty rather than for love. None of them possessed that innate aura of pleasure and satisfaction which emanated from Landon and his married set. Under his breath, Christopher mumbled, "I'll be damned if I make the same mistake as Weathersbee."

Launching himself into the night air, he hailed down a hack. "Eastside, sir. Ms. Lennox's establishment."

The driver nodded, and Christopher bounded into the vehicle. Relief that he was finally on his way to see Emma was slowly replaced with apprehension. There had been whispers at the office of her restricting visitors to family and clients. He was neither family nor a client.

His head lolled forward as he placed elbows upon his knees and clasped his hands together. He'd been an utter dolt for stating he'd leave her be. If the office gossip of her eyes being red and puffy was true, he'd beg her forgiveness for causing her to hurt. He wanted the opportunity to make things right.

The hack rolled to a stop. Jumping out of the vehicle, he flipped a crown up to the driver.

His greatest fear became a reality as Simon, one of Emma's guards, approached and said, "She's not at the shop."

He must have heard wrong. "It's one in the morn. Surely Emma is safely asleep in bed."

The blasted footman simply stared at him and shrugged. At another step towards Emma's shop, Simon shifted and blocked Christopher. "I assure ye, sir, she's not abed yet."

"Where is she then?"

"I can't tell ye. Would ye like fer me to hail ye another hack?"

Christopher shook his head and turned to begin the trek back across town to his townhouse.

Damnation. Where the hell was Emma?

CHAPTER FIFTEEN

A gust of wind pushed at Emma's back, forcing her to reach for the nearest solid tree trunk.

Blimey, it was cold. She tugged her cloak tighter about her. Glancing about, Emma searched the tree line for signs of Christopher's night watchman. She needed to time her approach with the change in guard. If she was caught, the Network would be abuzz. Gossip Christopher nor Emma could afford. Scanning the sky, Emma located the three-quarter moon set low to the south. Blast! She'd missed her chance—it was well past the midnight hour. Even after employing all the counterargument tactics Bronwyn had taught her, Emma couldn't convince Sebastian to alter his will. The man was a stubborn mule. Narrowing her eyes to locate the men on patrol, Emma slowed her breathing. She'd have to outsmart the Network guards.

Hugging the shadows, she crept through the gardens, bobbing and weaving around the neatly manicured hedges. She approached the back terrace, pebbles crunching beneath her slippers. She froze and scanned the area once more for the bloomin' guard. Two large black blurs moved fast in her direction. She picked up a stone no bigger than a small apple, and she threw it as far as she could in front of her. Emma dashed back to sneak down the stairs to the kitchen doors. Heart racing, Emma slipped through the entrance and rested her throbbing forehead against the inside kitchen wall. *That was too bleedin' close.*

She needed to see Christopher, regardless of whether he wished to see her. For four blasted days, she'd waited and wished Christopher would change his mind and come seek her out. But oh no, ever the gentleman, the man had kept his bloomin' word.

Pushing away from the door frame, Emma waited a moment, letting her eyes adjust to the darkness. The cold, empty kitchen was daunting compared to the last time she had visited during the bustling early morning hours. A strange yearning to stay rooted Emma to the spot. She should move. If she was caught, Emma would have to explain her actions to the Network elders. Would they believe her if she told them the only reason for her late-night visit was to seek out legal advice? No. They'd likely see through her flimsy excuses and wait for her to confess —she missed Christopher, and despite all the reasons she had formulated to stay away, she couldn't.

Emma willed her feet to move. She slipped past the footmen in the foyer and mounted the main staircase leading up to the upper floors. It would have been safer to use the servants' passageways, but whether it was courage from the drink Sebastian provided or Emma's desire to test her skills of going about undetected, she didn't care. It was the quickest route to her destination—the master bedchamber. The effects of the whiskey had Emma's mind foggy. However, scourging her memory for talk of the layout of Christopher's townhouse, she did recall Christopher's preference for sunsets. Looking down the corridor, Emma headed for the largest chamber that would face west.

Quietly opening the door to the chambers she hoped belonged to Christopher, Emma slipped into the room and paused for a moment. Without the aid of the moonlight, she carefully moved further into the pitch-black room. The familiar scent of Christopher, a mix of musty papers, ink, and wood. She was clearly in the right place. She stepped forward—

Arms twirled her about and wrapped about her like steel bands.

"Emma?"

The surprise in Christopher's voice almost had her giggling. Except the warmth of his body urged her closer. Barely louder than a whisper, Emma asked, "How did ye know it was me? It's darker than coal in here."

He ran his hand over her head and pressed her closer. "I know of no other woman who would dare come to my residence alone and in the dead of night."

Christopher stroked her back, melting away her stress. Instead of pulling away from the comforting gesture, Emma wrapped her arms about him and leaned her cheek against his hard, warm, bare chest. "Aye, I suppose it is a rather odd time of day to seek legal advice, but it was on me mind, and so I'm here." It wasn't the only reason, but it was the only one she was ready to admit to him at present.

He pulled her away from him by the shoulders. "Are you in trouble?"

She shook her head. But since she couldn't see anything, she assumed he couldn't either. "Nay."

"Stay here. I'll light a candle." He padded over to her left, and then the flame of the candle illuminated the room.

Her cheek was still warm from his skin. Emma's heart raced at the sight of him in only breeches. The small ridges outlining his stomach captured and retained her gaze. He was a barrister, not a laborer, yet he was muscled and toned as if he hauled bags of wheat for a living. As he came closer, his eyes raked over her from head to toe. The worry lines on his forehead were clear.

Instinctively, she rolled up onto her tiptoes and reached out to smooth the wrinkles away. "Ye need not worry. I'm fine."

He closed his eyes as if savoring her touch. She started to withdraw her hand, but he pinned her palm to his cheek. "This will sound bizarre given my hasty departure from your shop. But I've missed you."

Emboldened by drink, Emma said, "I've missed yer kisses."

Christopher lifted the candle closer. "Have you been drinking?"

"A little."

"Who was the scoundrel who plied you with wine?"

"Lord Hereford, and it was Scotch, not wine."

"Hereford?"

"Aye. He's the reason why I'm here."

Christopher shook his head. "Come, my dear, let's sit, for I'm not sure I understand."

She followed him to the enormous bed. He placed the candle on a table, picked her up by the waist, and settled her on the edge of the bed.

Standing in front of her with his hand on his hip, he said, "Now, let's start over. Why are you here?"

"I need ye..." She paused as his eyes widened. "I mean, I need yer help." She held in a sigh of disappointment as Christopher clasped his hands behind him. Emma's eyes tracked the thin trail of hair that disappeared into his breeches. She leaned closer.

"You mentioned you are in need of legal advice. How is Hereford involved?"

If she was quick about her request, then mayhap there would be time for a kiss or two before she would have to leave. "I can't read. I need ye to look over some papers fer me."

"Documents?" he mumbled.

"Aye. Hereford's will."

Christopher sank on the bed next to her. "Why would you want his will reviewed?"

"He claims he's arranged for me to inherit property and a sum of money, and this time, I'll not be able to avoid his generosity."

"This time?" He bundled her up and positioned her between his legs, so her back rested against his chest. Christopher's warm hands rested on her shoulders. "My dear, I apologize for not keeping up, but I've not slept in days. I need for you to tell me all of it so I may assist you."

Emma nodded. Safe in his arms, she took a deep breath. "Ye see, Hereford's papa wanted to atone for his own papa's misdeeds and bequeathed me a large sum of money. I asked Sebastian to give it anonymously to an orphanage run by the Network." Emma fiddled with the edge of her cloak. "I don't accept charity, especially from a bloomin' lord." She peeked up at him, and instead of pity in his kind brown eyes, she detected understanding.

He began rubbing her shoulders. She relaxed as his magical fingers eased the knots in her shoulders. Eyes closed, she said, "Tonight, Sebastian told me he has ensured I'd receive a cottage and funds upon his death. His solicitor assured him I'd not be able to gift the bequest to another."

"And this has you in knots. Your muscles are strung as tight as the strings on a violin." He shifted back towards the center of the bed and pulled her with him.

"What are ye doin'? I've still got me bleedin' boots on. I'll mess up yer nice bed."

He shimmied out from behind her, and in a flash, the man had divested her of boots and stockings. Settling himself on the edge of the bed, he grabbed her feet and began to rub her arches. She flinched as his thumb stroked the bottom of her foot, tickling the sensitive skin.

Scowling, Christopher stood once more and hauled

her to her feet. "You're a bundle of knots." He was annoyed with her.

He loosened the string that held her cloak in place and then, with one swift tug, removed the garment. Christopher inhaled as he took in the sight of her. "You are a beauty, Emma Lennox."

She stared at him, disbelieving her ears. Oh, the flare in his gaze wasn't from anger-—it was pure longing. He wanted her. The thrill of being coveted emboldened her. Her hands smoothed over his naked flesh, reaching up and linking her arms about his neck. She had been dreaming of kissing him. The sleepless nights tortured her days. Emma drew Christopher closer and brushed her lips against his lips. His tongue slipped between her lips, and she savored the heady taste of him in her mouth. Wanting more, Emma mimicked his bold movements, sticking her tongue out, and then pulled back, grazing her teeth along his lower lip. Christopher's deep, hungry growl mixed with her moan of delight. Open-mouth kisses were delicious.

Christopher withdrew and looked down at her. His pupils were dilated and irises ablaze. He pointed towards the top of the bed. "Up, my dear. Rest against the headboard."

She didn't know what he intended, but she was certain she wasn't ready to leave.

He knelt on the bed and arranged her skirts to lie just above the knee. "Who drafted Hereford's will?"

Bending her knees to her chest and tucking her legs

under her skirts, she protested, "Ye don't need to be touchin' me ugly feet."

"They are not ugly. Let me ease the knots from them." His hand moved to the edge of her skirts.

Emma blurted, "It's yer fault."

His hand stilled. "Mine?"

"Aye. Every time I'm near ye, me body gets tense." She stared as his lips curved into a deceptively alluring smile. She licked her lips.

"If it helps, you have a similar effect upon me." He placed his hand out palm up. "Please let me ease some of the tension."

She placed her foot in his hand and replaced her skirts above her knees. "Will ye help me?"

Christopher cupped the heel of her foot with one hand while his other snaked up to knead her calf. "Do you have any idea who Hereford sought out to draft his wishes?"

Swallowing a moan, she replied, "Nay."

"If perchance it was my brother, I'm afraid..." His hand stilled.

Emma opened her eyes and frowned. "Ye brother hasn't worked in an age."

"He still dabbles once in a while. Especially for those he deems friends." Christopher switched legs and repeated the magic that had Emma feeling like pudding. "Not to worry, there is always a loophole. I'll be happy to review once Hereford provides you a copy."

She scrambled off the bed and retrieved the folded sheets of paper from her cloak. Emma stood before a befuddled Christopher and held the relevant parts of Hereford's will out to him. "Here."

He took the paper from her hand and began to unfold it.

"Ye don't have to read it now." She took the papers and placed them on the table next to the candle. Turning back to face Christopher, she clearly saw the desire on his face. "Shall I pay ye now or later for yer services?"

"A kiss, for now, will do."

He wanted a kiss as payment. Her heart jumped in her chest. She placed her hands on his shoulders to steady herself. His heated gaze had her eager for his kisses. Pressing her lips to his, she wound her arms behind his neck and leaned closer, increasing the pressure of the kiss. When she raked her fingers through his hair, her whole body came alive. Christopher's hands remained at her waist. She craved his touch. For his hands to roam over her back like they had when they danced. His hands remained still, and so did his lips. She silently willed him to move, but he didn't respond. Seeds of doubt seeped into her—perhaps the kiss had quelled his desire for her rather than stoking it. She began to pull away, but Christopher groaned and crushed her to him, urging her to open for him. Yes. This was the sin she craved from him. With his help, she climbed up to straddle him on the bed. She didn't want the kiss to end and kept a tight hold on his hair. His engorged bulge nestled at her center. Instinctively she rocked her body closer.

Christopher pulled back. "I've said it before, and it

still holds true. You, Emma Lennox, tempt me like no other. But if you wish to remain an innocent..."

"And if I don't?" She placed a kiss on his cheek next to his ear. "What if I want to spend a night in yer bed?"

He captured her in a dark, hungry kiss. He released a growl. "If you stay, it shan't be for one mere eve." He nibbled on her collar bone.

"But I've got to git to work in the morn."

Christopher scowled down at her. "Let me be clear. If you stay and share my bed with me this night, we shall marry as soon as it can be arranged."

"Marry?" Emma narrowed her eyes. The man was serious, but so was she. "No one knows I'm here. I snuck past yer watchmen, and I can leave undetected. Ye needn't worry me dad will be after yer head." She reached behind and released the bow at the back of her dress, allowing her décolletage to gape loose.

Christopher ran a finger along the edge of her dress and over the tops of her breasts. "Before I ignore my better senses and agree to let you stay, tell me why you came here tonight."

"I made an error the other night. I pushed you away when really I wanted...I wanted you to stay. I'll not make the same mistake." She ground on him and circled her hips.

He dipped a finger between the valley of her breasts. "You know of my need to wed, and if you..." He gripped her hips and held them still. "My terms are non-negotiable."

"Me mum says everythin' is negotiable. Wot if I assist

ye in findin' a wife?"

"No."

"I seen maids bein' taken against a wall. Wot if we.."

"No."

"Ye're being difficult."

"And you are stubborn. Why do you object to marrying me?"

"I don't honestly know ye well enough."

"But you are willing to lie with me?"

"Aye." She smiled and pushed him to lay flat on his back. "I don't understand it, but I can't stop finkin' of ye and yer kisses. I keep hearing yer voice in me head. Thank goodness yer not a lord like yer brother, but ye will be a PORF soon enough, and then I'll not be able to enjoy the feel of yer lips on mine." She bent to partake in the devilish kisses.

Christopher managed to release the row of buttons at the back of her gown. Emma was thankful for the man's dexterity. The cold air hit the top of her back and shoulders as her dress fell open. Unafraid, Emma sat up and withdrew her arms through her sleeves. Reassured by Christopher's crooked smile, she reached behind her back for the ribbon of her stays. Her fingers grazed Christopher's as he assisted her in removing the horrid contraption, leaving her torso bare. His impassioned stare increased her own desire. Eager but uncertain as to what was to come next, Emma brought her hands to rest upon his sides. Mirroring her actions, Christopher's warm hands traveled down her ribs to settle at her waist. His touch had a possessive edge that made her feel coveted.

He urged her to her knees, gathered the freed material, and lifted her dress over her head. The rough fabric of Christopher's breeches rubbed against her naked thighs as she sank back down to sit upon him once more. Nervous but emboldened by her position atop of him, Emma found herself leaning forward to gaze into Christopher's burning eyes. Placing her hands on either side of his head, she lowered herself until their mouths were entangled. Her nipples pebbled as they grazed against his chest. He released a groan, halting her movements.

Christopher nuzzled her neck. "Now that I have you naked and in my arms, I certainly don't wish for you to leave, but unless you agree to be my wife, there'll be no more kisses. You enchant me, Emma."

She didn't want to leave. Simply being within a foot of the man, her entire body and mind entered a more relaxed, secure state. He made life exciting again. Her pulse began to race at the heat, radiating off of him. She needed to be closer. If she agreed, she would lose her shop, her freedom. She couldn't be seriously considering marrying the man. Or was she?

His warm skin was like a magnet pulling her body close. "I fink I've changed me mind." Christopher stiffened, but she rushed onto say, "It's not yer kisses I want more of, its ye that I want more of."

"Minx. I'll not take you until you agree."

She crossed her arms beneath her breasts. "Ye call *me* stubborn. Yer the most obstinate man I know."

"Why, that is one of the highest compliments I've

ever received, given you know my brother."

"Pfft." Her traitorous hand ran down his chest, and desire pooled between her legs. His manhood twitched beneath the taut material of his breeches. "What if we don't rub together right? Perhaps we should wait to discuss until after..."

"Hmmm... You have a point. To agree to a lifelong commitment before you know if you can experience pleasure at my hands would be rather risky on your part." He twisted, and Emma found herself the one lying on her back and him straddled across her thighs. He took in his fill of her body. "Decisions. Decisions. Decisions." He leaned forward. The inside of his wrists grazed the sides of her breasts as he planted his hands on either side of her. Ducking his head down, he kissed and suckled her breast before trailing his tongue across her chest to repeat the same delicious, torturous treatment to her other sensitive globe. Christopher emitted a low, feral growl. He kissed his way down the center of her body as he rested back on his haunches—hands trailing down her sides. Every inch of her body yearned for his touch.

Christopher sat up, a devilish smile on his fine features. She shivered. Whatever he had in store for her, she was sure it would remain forever burned in her memory.

He raised onto his knees and then moved to stand beside the bed. "Turn over and rest your head upon the pillows."

For once in her life, she didn't question. She did as he bid and rolled onto her stomach. Her cheek rested against cool, soft cotton pillows. A far cry from the lumpy pillow she slept on.

Instead of lying next to her upon the bed, Christopher padded over to a connecting room. He returned with a dark glass bottle in his hand. As he neared the bed, he removed the stopper and poured a liquid onto his hand. Her nose twitched at the aroma of roses. Scented oil. Her pulse increased with anticipation. He placed the open bottle and cap next to the candle. The bed slanted as he kneeled upon the bed, and Emma closed her eyes. She heard him blowing on his hands as he rubbed them together. Warm, slippery hands rested on her lower back, and then Christopher swept his hands up her back to massage the knots in her shoulders.

"Close your eyes and try to relax." He slowly kneaded his way down her back, dispelling each knot along the way.

She moaned as each muscle loosened and became lax.

He leaned down to whisper in her ear, "Do you recall my terms, my love?"

She nodded and mumbled, "Aye." She yawned and let her eyes close. She trusted this man for some odd reason that her mind couldn't fully comprehend. As his hands massaged down her back and along her thighs, she smiled. The heady sensation of being desired and treasured engulfed her and sent her heart soaring. And if he could pleasure her like this every eve, she'd willingly agree to marry him, but she wasn't ready to admit it just yet.

CHAPTER SIXTEEN

*C*hristopher's thumb rubbed over the rounded curve of Emma's bare shoulder. He'd normally be up and mentally preparing for the day. Except he couldn't focus on anything but the naked woman snuggled against his side, who was making soft chortles. He'd never invited a woman to his bed before, always preferring to leave women sated in their own beds. But Emma made him want to linger. His lips curved into a smile as he imagined waking up next to Emma each morn. Instead of focusing on the challenges the day might bring, as was his usual habit, Christopher began to envision days filled with adventures. For a life with Emma would be a far cry from boring.

Emma's eyes moved beneath her pale eyelids. What was she dreaming of? He wished she could read her mind. His intuition told him Emma hadn't merely arrived in the dead of night to seek out legal advice. She could have sought out Bronwyn's assistance, but she came to him. A spark of hope that Emma wanted him flared in his heart.

The faint streaks of sunlight filtering through his dark curtains marked the end of his time alone with his future wife. He'd not been surprised that Emma fell fast asleep as he massaged the knots from her beautiful body, but he hadn't expected her to sleep straight through the night. Ignoring the prickling sensation settling into his arm, he remained still and drank in her beauty. Emma was clearly exhausted, but if he was to sneak her out without detection, he'd have to rouse her and soon. He had locked the door as a precaution. His valet was rarely up before the sun, but Cannon had an uncanny ability to appear as soon as Christopher began to rise.

Reaching over with his free hand, he cupped Emma's rosy cheek. "Pet, it's time to wake. We need to get you home."

"Hmm..." Emma rolled over, pulling the bedlinens with her. In the struggle to free herself of the tangled sheet, her bare bottom nudged his hip. Shooting up to a sitting position, Emma blinked and looked about the room until her gaze fell upon him. "Blimey, wot time is it?"

A pretty pink blush colored her cheeks. His breath caught in his chest. Resisting the temptation to reach out and remove the blasted cotton sheet himself, he massaged his arm that tingled with pain. Blood rushed back into his fingertips, and his gaze wandered back to Emma.

She tugged the sheet up to her chin and stared back

at him. "Is it still early morn?" The corner of her mouth twitched as her gaze raked over his bare chest.

Christopher shifted to loom over her. He slowly bent his head, but it was Emma who reached out and drew his lips to hers.

Yes. This is exactly how he wished to spend every morn.

Tearing his mouth away from hers, he ground out, "We need to agree upon a date."

"A date for wot?" Emma pulled back and frowned at him.

"Our wedding."

She rubbed her eyes and narrowed her gaze. "Did I say I'd marry ye?"

"You agreed to my terms."

"But we didn't..." She lifted up the sheet and looked about. Sheet raised back up to her chin, she repeated, "But we didn't..." Emma wagged her prettily shaped eyebrows at him.

"I clearly stated that if you shared my bed for the eve, we were to be married."

"Nay." She shook her head and then, with a fierce look of determination, said, "We were to wed *only* if ye took me innocence."

"I don't believe that is what I said." He tilted her chin up so he could stare directly into her eyes. "Shall we agree to two weeks from today?"

She raised up onto an elbow and muttered something that sounded like *bloomin' brilliant barrister*, but he couldn't be sure for his attention was focused on rose-colored nipples that peeked over the edge of the sheet. She tugged at the linens once more.

"I never said I'd marry ye." Emma scooted away and jumped down from the bed. She wrapped the fine white bed linen tightly about her and searched the room for her garments.

"I'll tell you where your clothes are as soon as you give me an acceptable date."

"I told ye I'd help ye pick out a suitable wife."

"I want you."

"Why?"

It was a valid question. But how was he to explain what he instinctually knew was right?

He was a bloody barrister. He was supposed to be able to come up with arguments at a moment's notice. Instead of a carefully crafted proposition, he spoke from the heart. "Because from the moment you bumped into me dashing away from Landon's townhouse, my mind and body have been drawn to you. It's as if you dislodged something within me."

Emma stilled and turned. A small grin appeared before she crossed her arms and let out a loud *Hmph.*

She was pleased with his answer, despite her body language. He pressed on. "And there is the added benefit that if you marry me, you can enact the clause in Hereford's will that enables you to decline the rather large settlement he has generously provided for you."

Emma's eyes grew wide. Her hands dropped to her sides then were firmly planted on her perfectly rounded hips. "Ye're sayin' I can refuse the blunt if I git hitched."

He nodded. "Aye."

She tilted her head and stared at him for a moment. "Hmph." She slowly spun in a circle. A small grin appeared. "Where *did* ye put me clothes?"

He nodded in the direction of the connecting room. "I hung your dress in my changing chamber."

She walked soundlessly to the dark room.

He wanted to follow her, but he was struggling to formulate an articulate answer as to why she should marry him. Christopher hopped from the bed and began to pace. He needed her to agree to wed him. He wanted to have her back in his bed. He was going about matters all wrong. Why should *she* marry? She was independent and resourceful. She had no need for a man except that the only place she had appeared at peace was lying naked next to him.

He was a reasonable man. If she needed more time to recognize the benefits of becoming his wife, he'd be patient. He'd court her and show her how they complemented each other. Mayhap he'd draft provisions in the marriage agreements for her to retain control over her own funds. Damnation. He wouldn't be able to lawyer his way into marriage. His stomach clenched. He needed her. He'd have to convince her of their suitability. He didn't want her leaving his house without having her word that she'd marry him. His desire for her as wife was more than pure lust. He just didn't know what to name this burning desire to have her near at all times.

A few minutes later Emma reappeared, dressed, her hair held back by one of his blue silk cravats and wearing a look of pure determination. She had made up her mind. His heart pounded with anticipation.

She marched to stand before him and rested her hands on his waist. Head tilted up, she said, "I'll be busy fillin' orders for Bronwyn's ball this week. And I need another two to be ready. Will ye agree to three weeks?"

Why was she agreeing?

Uncertain if he wanted the answer, he said, "Yes. I shall visit your father today and have the license and agreements drawn up immediately." He reached out to cup her face. "I promise to be a good husband."

"Shall we seal our agreement with a kiss?"

Her wicked grin tempted him like nothing else. He replied, "I can't wait to make you mine."

Her hands slid up his chest, dislodging his hands from her face. Rolling up onto her tiptoes, she wrapped her arms around his neck. With her soft curves pressed into him, Christopher ran a hand down her spine until it came to rest on the curve of her bottom while his other hand threaded through her hair and guided her mouth to his. He kissed her softly.

Emma released a moan and opened for him as his tongue poked out to taste her. Pulling back for air, she inhaled deeply. She rested her forehead upon his chest. She whispered, "I best be off."

He didn't want her to leave him, but he'd garnered her promise to marry. He released his hold on her. She stepped back and gave him a wink. "Me dad comes to me shop every day around a quarter to eight." Swiveling on her heel, she made her way to the door.

He followed behind but pressed a hand against the door, delaying her departure. "I know. But I intend to obtain his blessing this morn." He waited until she turned to face him and then added, "Let me see you home."

"Are ye mad? I'll not have the Network gossipin' before ye speak to me dad."

Christopher was well aware of how very efficiently the Network spread information. Even Landon and Bronwyn hadn't managed to keep the news of the babe a secret. But he wanted to see Emma home safe. "The watch will be switching out soon, and you don't have the cover of darkness to help you go undetected."

"Ha. Ye have much to learn." She reached between her legs and pulled up her skirts, revealing her nicely shaped calves. Rather than exiting through the door, she marched to the window and peeked through the center slit in the curtains.

"You can't be serious. We are three stories up from the ground." He rushed to the window, but the woman was already out on a tree limb. He poked his head out and caught a glimpse of her small form shimmying down the tree and then ducking to skirt the low wall that led to the mews. Damn, she was fast and silent—and utterly remarkable. He turned to see the watchmen engaged in conversation, oblivious to Emma's departure.

"Is something amiss this morn, my lord?" Christopher jumped at Cannon's voice right behind him. Emma must have unlocked the door.

"No. I have a very important meeting this morn." He

ran a hand over his roughened jaw. "A good, clean shave today, Cannon."

A wide, knowing smile formed on his usually reserved valet's face. "Aye. I'll go fetch the strop."

Perhaps Emma hadn't been successful at escaping detection. He'd soon find out when he visited his future father-in-law.

CHAPTER SEVENTEEN

*E*mma crept up the back stairs of her parents' home, making her way past the bedroom she used to share with her half-siblings. She had grown used to sleeping alone. Her first month living away from the security of her parent's roof had been filled with nights of restless sleep—waking at every little creak of the shop. Emma rubbed her upper arms. It was cold most nights sleeping all alone, but last night in Christopher's arms, she had slept like a babe. Emma halted in front of her parents' chambers, wringing her hands. Her mind raced. Inhaling, she raised her hand to rap on the door. The thin wood door swung open before her knuckles hit.

"Emma." Her mum, already dressed for the day, quickly pulled Emma into the room. "Wot're ye doin' here?"

When dealing with her mum, it was best not to mince words. "I'm gettin' married in three weeks."

Her mum popped her head out of the doorway and

peered down the hallway. Closing the door as softly as possible, she leaned against the door and squinted at Emma. Her mum's gaze narrowed at the sight of Christopher's cravat that Emma had tied around her wayward tresses. Without a brush, it was the best solution she could manage at the time. No. She had wanted to take a little token from his closet, proof she hadn't dreamt it all up.

Her mum ran a finger over her cheek and then tilted Emma's chin up, forcing her to meet her mum's gaze. "Child, ye best explain. Start with who are ye marrying."

"Mr. Neale." Emma looked about the room. "Where is Dad?" Her dad always broke his fast with the family. A trickle of dread ran down her spine.

"He's been waitin' for ye at yer shop. If ye didn't see him, where have ye been all night?" Her mum grabbed her hands and squeezed. "Did the scoundrel seduce ye?"

Christopher was no rogue. She really should ensure the Network reports were revised. Emma shook her head. "No, Mum."

"But ye were in his bed?"

"Aye." Emma rushed to explain. "But Christopher was a complete gentleman. I'll say his sheets and mattress were rather fine. I slept like a babe."

Her mum released her hands and crossed her arms. "Hmph. Do ye want to marry him?"

With conviction, she answered, "Aye. I do."

"I thought you believed him to be a total louse, given his apparent lack of interest in his duties as a PORF. Wot changed yer mind?"

She certainly wasn't about to confess to her mum his kisses had anything to do with her agreeing to marry. Nor would she mention the details of Hereford's will. There was only one reason that would cease her mum's questions. "I fell in love with him." As the words tumbled from her mouth, the truth stuck her—she loved Christopher.

Her mum sat upon the bed and patted the mattress. "Mr. Neale is a handsome fella, I'll not deny, but are ye sure its love?"

"How can I be sure?" Emma obediently sat on the bed that wasn't as plush as Christopher's, but it was clean and familiar. With her forefinger, Emma traced the long stitches forming a simple floral design and waited for her mum to answer.

"It's difficult to say." Nothing rattled Emma's mum. Yet the woman she admired most in the world was nervously pleating the hem of the apron she wore. "When yer not with him, do ye fink of Mr. Neale?"

"Aye." Emma admitted and then added, "Sometimes I fink of his eyes, but mostly of his words and the clever little ditties he hums when he's concentrating."

"Ditties, you say." Her mum's gaze bored into her. "Wot d'ye feel when yer near him?"

Emma's cheeks heated. "Well, he makes me tummy all jittery, and I'm never cold when he's about."

"Hmm. Are ye able to chat with him?"

Emma smiled. This was an easy question to answer. "Aye, with as much ease as I can with ye."

Her mum wrapped Emma up in a hug. She pulled

back, and her mum rested her hands upon Emma's shoulders. "He makes ye happy then." Her mum gave her a gentle squeeze and smiled. "Yer muscles are not all knotted. Tis good. He's good for ye."

"Oh, aye. Mr. Neale can do wonders for me with his fingers."

Her mum's eyes went wide at her comment.

Emma ignored the strange reaction and said, "He used oils that smelt like roses and rubbed..." She pounded on her mum's back as she sputtered and coughed. "Mum, are ye all right?"

"Aye, ye need not tell me more. Ye shall marry Mr. Neale."

"Ye approve then?" Emma turned to hug her mum.

"If ye want him, I'll give him me blessin'."

Emma didn't understand what had caused her mum's cheeks to turn ruby red, but she nodded and said, "Thank ye, Mum. I fink Christopher will make a fine husband."

After a moment, her mum's coloring returned to normal, and in all seriousness, she pinched Emma's chin and said, "I'll not call him son until he receives the mark. Oh, luv, yer gonna be a PORF."

The truth of her mum's words sunk in. She was to marry a bloomin' PORF and, in turn, become one herself. *Blimey.*

Emma said, "I'll git the mark, but naught else will change. I'll still be yer daughter, and I'll remain..."

"Child. Wot are ye thinkin'." Her mum gave her a solid shake by the shoulders. "Everythin' must change."

Emma's body shuddered from excitement or from

fear; she wasn't sure which. A mere two weeks ago, she would have welcomed a change, but she hadn't imagined a difference in her life of this magnitude. "Everythin'? Why?"

Her mum looked at her like she was addled. "Wot do ye mean why?"

"I don't see how becomin' a PORF changes anythin'. I can still run me shop. Christopher ain't no lord."

"The Hadfield PORF duties are to seek and provide information to ensure the safety of the Crown; ye know this. Hadfields for generations have borne this responsibility. Once yer husband and ye receive the mark, Lord Hadfield is at liberty to send the two of ye on assignments. Ye can't be sittin' on the floor of yer shop sewing. Ye'll have other responsibilities. Not to mention ye're expected to produce a babe or two."

Emma saw stars. Her independence, her desires, her goals, all gone with a single night in the arms of a charming man. She loved him, yes, but she also loved her life, and the thought of choosing one over the other tore her very heart in two. Swallowing hard and blinking back tears, she whispered, "What have I done?"

Her mum withdrew a hankie from her pockets and handed it to Emma. "When I heard of Lord Hadfield's order for Mr. Neale to begin seeing ye, I told yer dad I was sure ye would fall for the handsome devil upon sight." Her mum smiled with a hint of pride. "But ye didn't. And by the reports from his staff and guards, ye have caused Mr. Neale to skip a few meals and nights of sleep. He's not had an easy time staying away from ye."

This was all new information to Emma. She took little comfort he had suffered during their time apart. The Network's methods of protection were, at times, wayward. Someone should have told her. She gave the unused hankie back to her mum.

Returning the clean material to her pocket, her mum said, "If me instincts are right, he's more aware than the Network gives him credit for."

Emma suspected the same. "What makes ye say that?"

"Hadfields are notorious for being able to charm the most jaded of souls. It is by no fair coincidence their lot are bred to be attractive to the eye and of a keen mind, and Mr. Neale is a Hadfield through and through."

Christopher was indeed enchanting—the man scattered her thoughts as soon as he appeared. "Do ye fink I made a mistake?"

"Matters naught wot I think. Does he know he must apply to the Council for yer hand?"

Emma groaned. "I forgot to mention it to him."

"Not to worry, yer dad will inform him." Her mum grinned, no doubt looking forward to questioning Christopher herself later. Ushering Emma to the door, her mum said, "Come along. Let's break our fast with the family before ye hole yerself back up in that shop of yers."

Emma followed her mum below stairs to the kitchens. She slowed at the patter of small feet behind her. Her siblings still had yet to master the art of moving about silently.

"Em, are ye goin' to invite us to the weddin'?"

She turned and knelt to face her youngest sibling, Thomas. The bloomin' walls of her family home were extremely thin, and her brother had mastered the skill of eavesdropping. "Ye will have to dress up fancy. Have a clean face, and ye'd have to be on yer best behavior."

Bouncing on his toes, Thomas said, "I promise to be good. I won't make a noise. I've been practicin'."

"Have ye now?" Emma asked.

Thomas gave a solemn nod and revealed his missing front teeth with a wide smile.

She had left the house to live at the shop when Thomas was born eight years ago, yet he remained the sibling she was closest to. "I see ye lost another tooth."

"Aye. Last week. Ye missed it." The small frown was a stab to her heart. Her brother was rarely ever cross with her, but her missing this milestone had obviously upset him. "If ye marry, will ye not come round no more?"

"Don't be silly. Of course I'll still come visit." The promise slipped from her lips before she thought better of it.

"Are ye sure?" Thomas had learned another talent, arching a single eyebrow. "Coz since Mr. Neale started a-courtin' ye, we ain't seen much of ye."

"I'm sorry, Tom. Nothing will change. I'll still come have supper once a week."

Dubious, he stuck out his pinky finger. She wrapped hers about his little finger and nodded solemnly.

Smiling once more, he wrapped his arms around her

neck. "Em, I've missed ye. Everyone else always treats me like a babe. Yer the only one who tells me the truth."

Emma's heart cinched. She shouldn't have said nothing would change, for that had been a lie. She would simply have to figure a way to make it the truth.

CHAPTER EIGHTEEN

*B*ounding out of his coach and up to the landing in front of Emma's shop, Christopher reached up to tug at his cravat that seemed to be tightening about his neck. Eager to see Emma, he pushed aside his fears of the conversation that must be had with her father. A mere two hours had passed since Emma had scrambled down a tree, but it seemed far longer under the extra attention his valet paid to shaving and dressing him. Cannon executed his duties with a precision and care that his valet claimed only befitting Christopher's upcoming meeting. Between the time Cannon had left to retrieve the strop and the time he returned, it was evident that the Network had learned of and dispersed the news of his plans to seek permission to marry Emma. His entire staff beamed with pride as Christopher walked through his townhouse on his way out.

Christopher's knuckles were about to hit the wood

frame when the door swung open, and Mr. Lennox's large form filled the space.

Through gritted teeth, Mr. Lennox asked, "Where's me daughter?"

The man's face was flushed red. Christopher had hoped to catch his future father-in-law in a fine mood, but like with most matters, Christopher would have to wrangle and charm his way through the situation. Peering over the stout man's shoulder, Christopher said, "I had assumed she was here with you." The coachman had advised Christopher he'd find Mr. Lennox at Emma's shop.

Mr. Lennox widened his stance and crossed his beefy arms. "She's not here. Wot d'ye want?"

It was a rather broad question—Christopher wanted the man's blessing to marry Emma. He wanted to marry posthaste. He wanted the mark of a PORF. He wanted a life of his choosing. He wanted to see to Emma's happiness. He wanted children. He wanted so much more, but first and foremost, he wanted Emma.

Matching Mr. Lennox's steely glare, Christopher said, "I would like to speak with you. Perhaps we could go inside?"

"Wot about?"

Surely the man had heard through the Network's communication channels Christopher's purpose. The twitch of his future father-in-law's lips gave the man away. Oh, Mr. Lennox knew why he had come—it was a challenge of sorts.

Playing along, Christopher looked about and puffed

out his chest stating clearly, "I wish to marry Emma and have come to—" He didn't finish his request, as he found himself stumbling backward.

Mr. Lennox's meaty hand was firmly planted in the middle of Christopher's chest as the man took a step forward, exiting the shop and closing the door behind him. "Ye need to seek the Council's permission first."

Christopher scanned his surroundings. His guards had moved into the shadows but were close by. Lowering his voice to a whisper, he asked, "The Network Council?"

His future father-in-law chuckled and then laid his heavily muscled arm over Christopher's shoulder. "Aye. It's not a far jaunt on foot. I'll take ye there."

An hour later, sweat dampened Christopher's collar. He glanced at Mr. Lennox. "You do know the way, don't you?"

"Of course I do."

Christopher wasn't certain. They had been alternating between a brisk pace and that of a tortoise. While Mr. Lennox was comfortable in a lawn shirt and breeches, Christopher was not enjoying the rare sun-filled morning. Christopher finally stopped to remove his hulking greatcoat. "How much further?"

Mr. Lennox grinned and said, "Oh, I reckon another block or two."

Christopher turned and searched for signs of the footmen following them. When they remained out of sight, Christopher asked, "Were you nervous when you sought permission to marry Emma's mama?"

"Gor—worst day of me life." Mr. Lennox grinned. "But I'd do it all over again."

Regaining his balance after Mr. Lennox nudged him in the side, Christopher wiped his brow with a handkerchief. "If I have to follow you around town all day for the opportunity to gain permission to marry Emma, I'll happily do it."

With a decided nod, the man said, "Ye'll do." Eyeing Christopher with a look of understanding, Mr. Lennox added, "Ye may have me blessin', but it's gonna take a lot more fer yer to charm the socks of the bloomin' Elders' Council."

Christopher didn't doubt the man's words and continued to trudge alongside his future father-in-law. Catching the slight shake of a guard's head in front of them, Christopher sighed and said, "You are awaiting a signal." The man's silence was confirmation enough.

He didn't have to wait much longer. Christopher spied the young footman Simon beaming a broad grin in Mr. Lennox's direction before disappearing behind a building. They came to a halt in front of Rutherford's jewelry shop. How fortunate—he'd be able to purchase a ring for Emma. Mayhap luck was on his side after all.

Mr. Lennox slapped Christopher's back, heartily, and said, "Good luck, lad." His future father-in-law winked and pushed open the door. "If ye manage to git their approval...and ye survive Cadby's torture, ye may call me Dad."

Christopher froze. Torture? Hadn't he suffered enough already? The agony of not knowing what the

Elders may demand of him as he traipsed about town was distressing enough. Although, the time spent in Mr. Lennox's company had allowed him to gain perspective. Emma was well worth any demand they may make of him.

Mr. Lennox gave Christopher another shove, and he stumbled into the shop. Righting himself, Christopher turned and asked. "Are you not coming?"

"Nay. I'm not a member of the council. Off ye go. They're expecting ye." Mr. Lennox turned and walked away, whistling a ditty as the door slid shut.

Staring at the closed door, Christopher wondered who "they" were. How many elders would he be facing?

Rutherford's booming voice came from the back of the shop. "Mr. Neale, I'd be much obliged if you would lock the door and turn the sign for me. We have been expecting you."

Christopher wasn't surprised that the old jeweler was a member of the Network Council. His store sign over the door displayed a rather intricate design of a harped angel—only slightly less elaborate than the one that adorned Emma's shop sign.

Rutherford continued, "We'll be with you in a moment. Might I suggest you peruse the cabinets at your leisure? I'm certain there is a ring that would suit."

Though he'd peered into each glass case , none of the wedding bands encapsulated Emma's unique personality. He reached into his jacket pocket and retrieved the half-size pencil and parchment he always carried. He'd sketch a wedding band that would reflect his feelings for Emma.

Instead of outlining a design, he found himself jotting down words.

Trust

Passion

Life

Yours

Forever.

A posy ring was the answer. If he was correct, Emma would prefer a plain gold band with a special inscription for her eyes only. He was no poet. He needed to choose the words wisely—but which ones would best convey his commitment and love for her?

Tapping the pencil against his lips, he bemoaned the limited vocabulary of a barrister when it came to feelings. From the corner of his eye, he caught Rutherford spying on him.

Tucking the pencil and parchment back into his jacket, Christopher turned to face the jeweler. "Rutherford. How long would it take for you to fashion a posy ring?"

"A gold band, no outer design with five or fewer words engraved, would take a few hours." Rutherford reached into a cabinet behind the counter and withdrew a tray of rings in various sizes and widths. The old man expertly palmed a few testing weights and sizes about his forefinger. After evaluating six or so, he selected one and handed it over to Christopher. "'Tis the one."

It was small and narrow, with little room for a message. "Five words, you say."

"Aye. Will that be an issue, sir?"

"No. Shall I provide them now or after our meeting?"

"After." Rutherford grinned and turned to lead him to the back room.

Christopher's stomach knotted. Unprepared for whom he was about to meet, he wasn't able to mask his surprise at being greeted by Emma's mother. If Mrs. Lennox was a council member, then Emma was a highly ranked member of the Network. Christopher inwardly groaned as Bronwyn's father, Cadby, came out from the shadows and stood behind Mrs. Lennox.

Lord Waterford appeared next and stood to the right of Mrs. Lennox. "Christopher, welcome. Due to the importance of the matter to be discussed, the council deemed it necessary to convene at this rather odd hour. However, that precludes two members who are currently at work. Both have proxied their votes to Mrs. Lennox."

"I apologize for the inconvenience. I'd be willing to return at a more convenient time if it would be preferred."

Mrs. Lennox stepped forward. "Ye're not to see Emma unless terms have been agreed to." The woman moved to sit at the head of the table, motioning Christopher to be seated to her right.

He slid into the chair, and the others took their seats. Lord Waterford, the only familiar friendly face, sat opposite him.

Hands clasped resting on the table, Mrs. Lennox calmly said, "Ye shall arrange to have the banns read at our parish, not yers. Fer the next three weeks, ye're to dine with our family on Wednesdays. And no more sneakin' about at night; ye'll court me Emma proper."

Christopher released a sigh of relief. As far as demands went, the ones made so far were easy to fulfill. Except he found Mrs. Lennox's stipulation to dine with Emma's family for only three weeks peculiar.

Before he could utter his agreement to the requests, Lord Waterford added, "The council also respectfully requests you see to it that Emma agrees to limit her services to only those listed." He pushed a piece of paper towards Christopher.

Christopher scanned the features of the members of the council. Not one of them appeared happy with the request, but all seemed resolved. He looked to Mrs. Lennox. "Emma's shop is everything to her. It should be hers to run as she pleases. I understand as a husband, I'd legally have the right to make such an absurd demand, but...it will be impossible to do as you ask without hurting Emma."

Mrs. Lennox stiffened in her seat, and her brows swooped down into a fierce frown. "You will have to figure out a way."

He was willing to do anything to secure their consent, but to agree to Emma relinquishing control over her shop was like asking him to give up the firm. The demand was unthinkable.

Lord Waterford cleared his throat. "We humbly *request* that you, as a member of the Hadfield line, seek your brother's permission for you and Emma to escort a contingent of Network members to America. Our intent is that they will remain and establish a base there so we may fulfill our duty to support all PORFs. It will allow you to take Emma on an adventure and, allow time for the two of you to adjust to your new roles."

Christopher mumbled, "Madness. Utter madness." Becoming a PORF appeared to be a double-edged sword. He wanted to fulfill the duties of a PORF as the men in his family had done for generations. But to hurt the woman he loved in order to carry out those duties—he couldn't do it. There must be another way. And as Mrs. Lennox stated, he'd have to figure out a way.

The man he thought a friend stared at Christopher hard. After moments of silence, Lord Waterford sighed. "If you don't believe you can meet our wishes, we shall have to refuse permission to wed Emma. Only a man willing to take on these tasks is worthy of our Emma's hand."

Damnation. While the voyage to the eastern shores of the New World was fast becoming routine, the seas were still littered with pirates. It was not a short jaunt to Europe and back. This request would require significant planning, many weeks at sea, and then many more months once they were upon land to safely establish and infiltrate a city. It was an enormous challenge. And hadn't he privately wished for change and adventure only a few weeks ago? There was no other woman of his acquaintance that he would want by his side to assist him, but what of Emma's wishes?

When Lord Waterford placed his palms flat upon the table as if he was preparing to leave, Christopher stalled the man's actions by saying, "Very well. I agree to your terms." After all, he'd vowed to do whatever they asked.

With a wide smile, Mrs. Lennox whispered, "Ye should have tried to negotiate."

"Emma is too valuable to me to risk the council's wrath."

"Welcome to me family." She patted his arm. "I shall do me best to ease things with Emma, but yer brother and the journey across the seas, that ye'll have to do on yer own."

"I appreciate the support, but I shall fulfill *all* requirements on my own."

Mrs. Lennox stood, and the men followed. Last to rise, Christopher caught Waterford staring at the parchment still sitting upon the table.

He unfolded it, expecting a long list of ladies' names. Instead, there was only one name, and a peculiar one at that. *Eliza Suttingham.* Damnation. The woman's name meant either he was to bring Tobias, Lord Burke, the third PORF family back home to England, or the journey was intended to be more permanent. His mind began to whirl with possibilities and ramifications. Stomach and head in turmoil, Christopher simply blinked when Waterford slapped an arm about his shoulders.

His friend gave him a little shake. "Do not fear. I'm at your disposal should you need assistance."

"My thanks." Christopher waved the note in front of Waterford. "Who decided upon this?"

"I'm not at liberty to say. I might suggest you have tea

with your dear sister-in-law, Countess Hadfield, this afternoon."

Yes, an afternoon with Bronwyn would be a grand idea. But he needed to speak to her alone. Turning to Waterford, Christopher asked, "I could do with your help."

Instantly Waterford replied, "I'm happy to assist."

"I need you to keep my brother occupied for a few hours."

The man's eyes widened and lit up with excitement. "Hmmm...what do you suggest?"

Christopher loved his brother and inwardly flinched at the idea of Waterford inflicting physical harm to Landon, but he needed a solid two hours to discuss matters with Bronwyn. "An afternoon at Gentleman Jacksons?"

Grinning, Waterford said, "Perfect. Hadfield needs to be knocked on his arse every now and then. I'll happily volunteer to do it. How long do you need him gone?"

Christopher suspected Waterford still had not forgiven Landon for vying for his lady's hand in marriage, not that Lady Mary ever seriously considered Landon's suit.

Regretting making the suggestion, Christopher asked, "Why?"

"Well, if I knock him out right away, it won't give you much time with Countess Hadfield. I think I shall let him get a punch or two in."

"If you wouldn't mind. But I'll warn you, while you

have been up holed up in Scotland with your wife, Landon's been practicing with Archbroke."

"Hmph. Don't worry, you'll have plenty of time to discuss matters with your dear sister-in-law. However, I do expect you to have whatever is needed to carry out the promises you made here today." Cracking his knuckles with glee, Waterford left the room.

There was only one last task before he took his own leave. He tore off the bottom half of the parchment with Miss Suttingham's name on it and placed it between his lips, while he folded the remaining half with the woman's name on it and tucked it into his breast pocket. Withdrawing his pencil from his jacket, he took the parchment from his mouth, bent over the table, and scribbled the words, *me kisses are fer ye.*

Grinning, he left the room and as he passed Rutherford the note. "I'll be at my brother's townhouse; have it delivered there."

Without looking at the note, Rutherford said, "It will be done."

Christopher strode down the path with a new purpose. Anything for Emma.

CHAPTER NINETEEN

*E*yes trained on the center of the Hadfield butler's back, Emma followed the man she'd known since childhood and whose family had served the Hadfields for generations.

Sweeping the drawing room door open for her, he whispered, "My felicitations on your betrothal. We are proud of ye."

Emma met the old man's gaze that shone bright with pride. "Me thanks. I hope Christopher survives his meetin' with the council."

Bronwyn's quick, slippered footsteps were nearing, and Emma braced herself for an embrace. Except her best friend didn't engulf her in a hug from behind; instead, the lady grabbed her hand and tugged her into the room. The soft click of the door echoed through the large drawing room.

Face-to-face with her best friend's scowl, Emma

masked her disappointment. "I've come to share the news of my engagement to Christopher and to—"

Bronwyn narrowed her gaze, squeezed Emma's hand, and said, "While I'm overjoyed at the news, I'm befuddled as to exactly how this all came about."

"Ye don't look happy."

Releasing Emma, Bronwyn gracefully sank down into a chair and waved to the settee. "Sit."

Emma perched herself on the edge as she had last time she visited. "Wot has ye in such a foul mood this morn?"

"Your mum paid me a visit on her way to the council meeting. Before Christopher arrives, I need to know why you agreed to marry."

Since her mum had already popped by, Emma repeated the reasoning she gave her mum. "I love him."

"Emma Lennox, you just met Christopher not long ago. Are you sure there is no other reason?"

Of course her best friend wouldn't simply accept a declaration of love. Using the tactic of avoidance, one of Bronwyn's favorite devices to deflect her opponents, Emma said, "The other reason I'm here is to tell ye I've changed me mind, and I'll be attendin' yer bloomin' ball after all."

Hereford had asked for her assistance, and Emma hadn't the heart to refuse. She'd given her word to watch out for Arabelle at the blasted event. Hereford was a fine negotiator. It was no wonder he excelled as an advisor to the King and Prinny. A burst of pride radiated within Emma and her lips curved into a smile.

Bronwyn leaned forward and pinned Emma with her gaze. "Why do I suspect that your change of heart about the ball and your betrothal are somehow interrelated?"

"I've no clue wot goes on in that head of yers. Aren't ladies supposed to offer tea or refreshments?"

The faint sound of Christopher's footsteps in the hall had Emma jumping to her feet, nearly tripping over her own blasted skirts. "Christopher has arrived."

Bronwyn looked to the door. "How do you know it is Christopher and not my husband?"

"First, the staff scurry when Landon is about. Second, Landon favors Hessian boots, which have a heavy heel, and Christopher has taken to wearing the new shorter-heeled boot designed by Wellington and made by Hoby. Does becoming pregnant make ye deaf?" Emma moved quickly to stand near the far window. Her feelings for Christopher remained a jumbled mess. She wasn't prepared to see her betrothed. Not having time to fully sort through all her mum had shared with her this morn, Emma instinctively slipped back into the shadows

"Not at all. You have always had better hearing than I."

Emma muttered, "Or now ye are a lady, ye're getting' soft and not payin' attention to wot's goin' on?"

Bronwyn snapped back, "I heard that."

Emma positioned herself so the drape partially concealed her form but allowed her a clear view of the door and her friend. Bronwyn was carefully arranging both her skirts and her features. The door flew open, and Christopher marched in.

Bent to give Bronwyn a hug, he asked, "How are you feeling today?"

Christopher was dressed in a royal blue jacket with a plain white waistcoat and cravat. The ends of the navy cravat that no doubt went with his ensemble but was instead in Emma's hair brushed against the back of her neck. She clutched the edge of the drapes. The urge to be near him was at odds with her training to remain undetected.

Bronwyn's smile was strained. "I'm well."

"Liar."

"I am not." The ladylike curve of Bronwyn's lips was gone, replaced with a grin that held a challenge. Emma wanted to warn Christopher to be careful, but Bronwyn released a heavy sigh and said, "It's not my pregnancy that has my stomach in knots this morn."

Blimey. They had been raised to be mistrustful of others, and it was a rarity that Bronwyn ever let her guard down. Yet Christopher, in a matter of moments, had disarmed Bronwyn and had the woman confessing the truth. Hadn't he charmed Emma just as easily? Egad. She would need to be cautious, or she, like Bronwyn, would lose her edge.

Bronwyn reached into her skirts and handed Christopher a box. "This arrived for you hours ago."

Christopher inspected the box, but his features gave Emma no indication of what might be inside. "Perfect." He placed the box on the side table and flopped onto the settee as if he hadn't a care in the world.

Clutching her hands in her lap, Bronwyn asked, "Did

you meet with the council?"

He rubbed the back of his neck. "Aye, and I should like to share with my fiancée what was discussed as soon as she decides to cease attempting to blend into the damned curtains and come join us."

Bronwyn whispered, "Old habits are hard to break. Give her some time."

Emma's nostrils flared as she inhaled and walked directly to stand before her betrothed. Glancing down at Christopher, all her anger evaporated at the sight of his teasing smile. Tamping down the urge to kiss the smirk off the man's face, Emma asked, "Did ye get the council's permission?"

Christopher patted the space next to him. "They have requested I see to a number of tasks before and after we wed." He reached for Emma's hand and rubbed his thumb over the top of her knuckles. Turning to address Bronwyn, he said, "Was Landon present when you met with the council?"

What the devil was going on? Emma sank to the settee, and Christopher pulled her closer to him. Worried that the council had made impossible demands, she settled in close as an act of support.

Bronwyn's eyebrows arched. "My husband had already left when Mrs. Lennox arrived and requested I attend an impromptu council meeting prior to meeting with you."

"Would care to explain the reasoning behind their requests?" All the color faded from Bronwyn's face as he pulled out a piece of ripped parchment from his breast pocket. "In particular, why Emma is to provide her services exclusively to this one woman?"

Emma couldn't believe her ears. The council was restricting her clientele to one. "Who?"

Bronwyn raised her chin and answered, "Miss Eliza Suttingham."

Emma blurted, "Who on God's green earth is that?"

Her best friend calmly said, "The woman who Tobias, Lord Burke, is in love with and the reason why he has abandoned his duties here as PORF and left for New York."

"Is that your hypothesis as a PORF or a former Network member?" Christopher's question caused Bronwyn to flinch. It was odd to see her normally unflappable friend flustered.

"It's not a theory. It is a fact."

"So Lord Burke informed my brother that he has forsaken his oath to carry out the Burkes' family duty to protect the royal family."

"Well, not exactly. Prior to leaving, he did not share his plans with any of the PORFs." Bronwyn's eyes darted to Emma.

"Hmph." When Emma's huff failed to draw Christopher's attention, she moved her free hand to rest upon Christopher's knee. His gaze fell upon her hand before it traveled up to meet Emma's. "The Network elders were informed that when Lord Burke departed for the New World, he instructed his steward to sell everything that wasn't entailed and left specific instructions as to how to disburse the funds to those in his service."

Christopher glanced back at Bronwyn. "Then explain why *I* am to convince *your husband* it is prudent for a retinue of Network members be sent to follow Lord Burke?"

Emma didn't care for Christopher's tone. Her friend was in a challenging position. Like Emma, Bronwyn had been raised to take a seat at the council table when the time came. But now, Bronwyn was a PORF and no longer privy to all the Network's workings and discussions. Emma spoke before Bronwyn. "What exactly did the council task you with?"

Christopher shifted to face Emma fully. "What would you say to traveling across the ocean to the New World for a spell, after we wed?"

His question slowly registered in her mind. She peeked over his shoulder at Bronwyn, whose eyes were trained on the tips of her shoes that were poking out from beneath her skirts.

Bronwyn stood and said, "Excuse me, I shall go see about arranging tea." Her friend practically ran to the door and closed it as she left.

Emma raised her hand and cupped Christopher's cheek. She had a plethora of questions, but she saw the worry in his eyes. Leaning forward, she tilted her head slightly and pressed her mouth to his. She ran her tongue along his bottom lip. He opened for her. Emma kissed him with a passion she hadn't realized had been slowly building all the while she sat next to him. A deep groan mixed with her soft mews until she pulled back for air.

"Has the council tasked ye to oversee the safety of the Network members who are to go?"

"Aye."

"Did they order me to accompany ye?"

"Nay. They requested that ye limit your services to Miss Suttingham."

"Who resides in America."

"That is true."

"Are ye goin' to convince Lord Burke to return to England?"

"I've had the opportunity to work with the Suttinghams on a number of occasions since the trade embargoes were lifted. From my dealings with Miss Eliza, she is a woman who shares our strong beliefs in fulfilling one's duties." Christopher pulled her on to his lap. "I've no idea what Lord Burke's plans are, but I intend to find out."

"Ye didn't answer me question." Emma wrapped her arms around his neck and stared into his eyes. "Ye don't need to prove to me ye're the best barrister about. I know ye are. Will ye jus' answer me straight?"

Christopher grinned. "I've no plans to persuade anyone to do anything they don't want to."

She wasn't certain if they were discussing Lord Burke or whether she was willing to accompany him.

He leaned his forehead against hers. "I simply don't believe Lord Burke has indeed decided not to return. Mayhap he is uncertain as to how long it will take him to convince Miss Suttingham to marry him. She's not the trusting sort, and there very well may be vile rumors that have reached foreign soil regarding Lord Burke's sordid past and his recent actions."

Emma's heart cinched at the possibility Lord Burke's affections might not be returned. How painful that would be. Warm and secure in Christopher's lap, she didn't want to move and sever the moment.

But Christopher pulled back and placed a chaste kiss upon her forehead. "What do you think about venturing across the ocean with me?"

Miss Suttingham wasn't the only one who wasn't the trusting sort. To leave her family, the security of the Network, and place her full trust in Christopher, a man she was only beginning to understand, was too much. Her heart ached. "I want to marry ye, but I can't leave." Her stomach clenched, and she shook her head. She wasn't ready to embark on this challenge. She couldn't give up the one thing she could call all her own. Not yet.

Her mum's words, uttered repeatedly over the years, rang in her head—*Ye're sworn to abide by the wishes of all PORFs.* What had she done? Christopher wasn't technically a PORF until he received the mark. She wasn't bound by her oath—was she? Blast. Why had she agreed to marry a bloomin' Neale? The skin along the back of her neck prickled. Christopher ignited a passion she couldn't ignore. He created within her a sense of caring for a man she'd not experienced before. Grappling with her thoughts, she didn't notice that Christopher had unwrapped her arms from about his neck and settled her next to him on the settee until she was a good arm's length away from him.

Voice gruff, Christopher said, "I shan't force you to do anything that displeases you. I myself spent most of the day pondering the request. I fully understand how scary and daunting it is to even think about leaving one's family for an unknown time period. But this is an important mission. The PORFs need to know for certain what Lord Burke's intentions are. And the Network elders believe it imperative Lord Burke be protected until he denounces his oath as PORF."

Emma's shoulders rolled forward. "Do ye still wish to marry me?"

"Aye, most definitely. You can't get out of your promise to wed me that easily. If you choose to remain, we shall begin your lessons immediately."

"Lessons?"

Christopher grinned. "I must teach you how to read and write so we can correspond."

She tried to return his smile, but her lips refused to turn up at the corners. "I need to return to my shop." Emma stood, and Christopher did too. Before she could do something insane like plaster herself to the man, Emma twirled and fled.

Never before had she wished for a different life.

She loved her shop. Her family needed her support.

Halfway to the foyer, Bronwyn caught Emma by the upper arms. "Where are you going?" Her friend's eyes filled with worry.

"I must return to my shop."

"Sarah and Maude are capable. They can look after the orders for the afternoon."

"I'm not talkin about today. Ye don't understand…"

"Emma. I know what the council has asked of Christopher. Landon will hate the idea of Christopher venturing so far from home. Christopher will need his wife by his side."

"But wot of me family and the shop?"

"Don't you trust Landon and me to care for your family?" Bronwyn let her hands fall to clasp Emma's. "You know there are plenty of us willing to help with the shop. It will be here. Your husband will not."

Emma shook her head.

Bronwyn released Emma and took a step back. "I shan't say more. But promise me you will think upon what really makes you happiest. Knowing Christopher, he will support whatever you decide. But the Americas is a long journey from here. I'd not want Landon to be that far from me."

"Was it not ye who slept in me bed but a few months ago, after runnin' away from yer husband?"

"Oh aye, that was me, and I'm telling you don't make the same mistake I did. If you love Christopher, which I suspect you do—you had best be ready to board the ship alongside him."

Emma tucked her stubborn chin to her chest and left her friend's side. Marching out of the Hadfield townhouse, Emma concluded Bronwyn was right, but her heart ached at the thought of leaving her family. She needed to return to the shop. Sorting buttons would detangle the knots in her brain.

HIS SISTER-IN-LAW ENTERED the drawing room with a dark scowl upon her face. He wasn't ready to discuss matters with her and turned back to look out the window, hoping to catch one more glimpse of Emma before she hopped into the faux hack his brother had purchased for Emma's use. He didn't blame Emma for not wanting to leave. There wouldn't be anyone across the ocean willing to take such preposterous actions merely to see to their safety or well-being. They would be in a strange land with few acquaintances and a small contingent of supporters. Except they would have each other, but only if Emma agreed to accompany him.

Bronwyn came to stand next to him. "You're going to charm Emma into going with you, aren't you?"

Christopher continued to stare out onto the street. "Don't you ever tire of meddling in others' lives and of others interfering in yours?" He certainly did.

His sister-in-law leaned a little further to peer out the window. "All my life, it is how things have been done. The Network attempts to only involve themselves for the benefit of the whole, not one individual. However, I can't say I've seen PORFs behave in the same manner throughout the years."

"Ha. This coming from a PORF." His breath caught in his chest, hoping Emma would turn to see him in the window. Without a backward glance, she bounded up into the vehicle that would see her safely delivered to her shop. He exhaled, releasing his disappointment.

"A PORF who only received the mark seven weeks ago." Bronwyn rested a hand upon his arm. "You know the council would not have requested your assistance if they didn't believe it imperative."

"But would they have sought out my aid if I hadn't been seeking their permission to marry Emma?"

Bronwyn left his side to resume the seat she had occupied earlier. "I have no idea what would or could have been done if circumstances had been different. However, I'm certain the council will not be happy to hear you are willing to leave Emma behind."

He wasn't thrilled about the idea of Emma remaining in London either, but he wouldn't force his betrothed to accompany him. Christopher meandered over to the table and slipped the box that contained Emma's ring into his pocket. Taking a turn about the room, Christopher contemplated all that must be done prior to the wedding and his departure.

Pausing to stand before Bronwyn, he already regretted what he was about to ask of his sister-in-law, but it had to be done, "Will you assist me in ensuring Landon stays out of Lord Weathersbee's way and allows the man to handle matters at Neale & Sons while I'm away?"

Bronwyn nodded. "How long do you expect to be gone?"

"Mayhap six months, but it's questionable whether I'd survive that long without Emma." Damnation, the truth was he couldn't bear the thought of leaving without her. But what was he to do?

CHAPTER TWENTY

*M*ounted upon his horse, Christopher slid a glance at his brother, who sported a rather nasty gash above his right eyebrow. Having already spent most of the day away from the office, Christopher decided to write the entire day off and accepted Landon's invitation for a ride. He'd hoped a hard ride and some fresh air would help provide clarity as to how best to go about declaring his love for Emma. He did not expect to be trotting along the crowded path in Hyde Park. "Why are we here?"

"I'm attempting to gain intel, *and* I needed to speak with you."

Christopher wasn't in the mood for one of his brother's lectures, nor was he ready to even attempt to discuss the Network's requests.

Landon's brows angled sharply down. "Waterford informed me you have sought out the Network Council's approval to wed Emma."

Lips thinned into a straight line, Christopher held in the expletive that threatened to burst from him in a roar. Waterford had no right to tell Landon. He'd planned to tell his mama and Landon at supper later that evening. However, he'd not have the pleasure of sharing the good news with his own family. His chest constricted. How to explain to his mama that he was to marry, receive the mark of a PORF, and then set sail for America—mayhap without his bride. His mama had always provided sage advice, and he'd hoped she'd be able to guide him. The knot about his heart tightened. Half a world away, he'd not have a family. But he'd also not have the meddling of well-intentioned friends like Waterford.

Landon stroked his horse's neck to settle the beast as they were forced to come to a halt. "Are congratulations in order or not?"

He wasn't ready to answer. Christopher asked, "Who are we spying on today?"

"Lord Markinson."

"Whatever for?"

"The scoundrel apparently has been acting out of character of late and even paid a visit to Rutherford's."

Good gracious. To think the Head PORF had nothing better to do than gallivant about town to conduct investigations into the behavior of a gentleman. The ton rumors were far more extravagant than Markinson could ever possibly achieve, but the man had never bothered to attempt to squelch the audacious gossip. He tilted his head in Landon's direction. "And you are concerned...why?"

"If Lord Burke doesn't return, then we must find another family to fill the vacancy."

Christopher scoffed. "*If?* Or have you already decided for Lord Burke? And why not Hereford? He is already appointed advisor to the King and Prince Regent. The official role held by the Burkes previously."

Lowering his voice, Landon answered, "Hereford too is under consideration. However, times are changing, and so must the PORFs and the Network."

Hmm. Christopher didn't disagree with Landon, but in his experience, most people feared change. Fear. Emma was scared. It was the only reasonable explanation for her hesitancy to accompany him.

The gaggle of carriages was moving again. Kicking his heels, Christopher moved his steed forward slightly ahead of Landon. When his brother drew even, Christopher said, "I request your blessing to escort a Network contingent across the ocean to support our missing comrade Lord Burke."

They rode in silence. Landon's gaze remained forward as if he hadn't heard Christopher. However, he knew his brother was ruminating upon the request. Landon never did anything in haste.

Further along, headed towards them on the opposite side of the path, Christopher spied their target. Markinson rode alongside a carriage that conveyed his two sisters, both a decade younger than himself. The girls were wide-eyed and tittering behind their hands. Had it already been a year since Markinson's mama died? It was clear as day to Christopher the reasons behind Markinson's reform. He wanted his sisters to marry well. Thoughts of marriage had images of Emma floating before him. Oblivious to the passing crowd, Christopher's thoughts were on the woman he wished was riding next to him. His mount slowed, matching his brother's pace.

Landon nodded. "Hereford. Lady Arabelle. You are a vision this fine afternoon."

"Lord Hadfield. Mr. Neale, how lovely to see you both out today." Arabelle had greeted them both, but her gaze was focused upon Christopher.

Christopher looked past Lady Arabelle to find Markinson glaring at them. He didn't blame the man for being irritated—holding up traffic was extremely annoying.

Nodding to Arabelle's brother, Christopher said, "Hereford."

Turning to smile at Arabelle, Christopher caught the heightened coloring in Markinson's cheeks. The man wasn't angry at being delayed. No, the blaze in the man's eyes was a sign of jealousy. Christopher chuckled. Both he and Arabelle had been disappointed that their well-timed discreet kisses to raise Markinson's ire a year ago had failed to prompt the man into action. It appeared he might have had a change of heart recently. Guilt clogged Christopher's throat. He was a damn hypocrite. He had interjected himself and played a part in trying to bring another man up to snuff—interfering, like a meddlesome marriage-minded mama, in another man's life. No one should be manipulated into making life-altering decisions.

Landon must have seen his discomfort and said, "Lady Arabelle, how observant of you. It's terribly hard to convince Christopher to leave the office these days."

The woman finally withdrew her gaze from Christopher, but her features were marred by a slight frown. "I'm looking forward to finally meeting Countess Hadfield. I shall see you *both* at the Hadfield ball?"

His brother's smile brightened. "Of course. I wouldn't dare upset my dear wife."

Landon gave Christopher a sharp look. There was an underlying message, but at present, Christopher was keeping a close eye on Markinson, who grew more irate by the moment.

With a curt nod, Christopher said, "A good day to you both. Hereford. Lady Arabelle." Urging his mount forward once again, Christopher avoided Markinson's angry glare as they passed by seconds later.

Chuckling, Landon slapped Christopher on the shoulder. "My thanks, brother. I have all the intel I sought. Let's return to my townhouse for a glass of brandy, shall we?"

He shook his head. "Not unless you are planning on providing me with your consent to travel abroad."

"Let's not discuss this here. Perhaps in my library would be preferable."

"Brother, there is nothing to deliberate. It is either a yes or a no." Christopher had never spoken to Landon in such a curt manner. He didn't have time to debate the issue. If Landon would not give his endorsement, he'd speak to the patriarch of the other PORF family, Theo's husband, Lord Archbroke, and gain his backing.

"Don't bother thinking about approaching Archbroke. I'm Head PORF, not he."

Blast. Christopher hated that Landon knew him so well. "There is much to do, so please give me your answer."

Landon sighed. "Answer me this first. Do you plan on returning?"

"If Emma refuses to accompany me, then yes, without a doubt. If she changes her mind and allows me to take her on an adventure, I can make no guarantees."

"You would go without Emma?" Landon's horse whinnied and moved off the path. His brother's thighs must have twitched at his outburst.

Christopher maneuvered his mount around to rejoin Landon. "I don't wish to, but I will not force her to come along."

Landon stared at him as if he didn't recognize who he was. Christopher waited. Unlike others, Landon was not intimidated by silence. After the count of forty-five, Landon urged his mount towards Christopher.

Embracing Christopher in an awkward hug, Landon whispered, "You have my blessing and best wishes, little brother."

Christopher beamed, and the sun shone a little brighter through the clouds. The uncertain future that had weighed on his shoulders all day was no longer a burden but a ray of hope. If Emma saw the future in the same light, then all would be well. But what if she didn't?

CHAPTER TWENTY-ONE

A pea whizzed past Emma and miraculously landed inside her little brother's wide-open mouth. Thomas's broad grin had Emma laughing. She hadn't felt much like smiling since leaving the Hadfield townhouse. Sarah and Maude had shooed her from the shop after Emma had accidentally pinned the wrong pattern to a fine cream-colored silk. Thankfully she hadn't taken her shears to the material before Maude had caught the mistake. Distracted by thoughts of Christopher and his plans to leave England, she had wandered about the penny street markets until she found herself in front of her parents' house.

Thomas swallowed the hearty bite of bread he'd managed to stuff in his small mouth. "Em, are ye goin' to eat yer cheese?"

Emma picked up a slice of her brother's favorite cheese from her full plate and handed it to him. Her mum shook her head but grinned at the same time.

Emma scanned the other smiling faces about the table. Her whole family was happy. She was to marry in a few weeks and a little in awe that she was to become a PORF. Her sisters had badgered her to bring Christopher home to meet them until her mum told them her betrothed had already promised to join them for supper every Wednesday. Her mum failed to mention it was only until he departed for the New World, but Emma understood there was no need to dampen their spirits.

The sisters rose and collected the empty food platters while her brothers gathered the dishes. Her mum placed a hand on Emma's arm. "Let yer sisters and brothers take care of cleaning up. Yer dad and me want to have a chat with ye. In the parlor."

Emma rose and followed her mum into the cozy room, a quarter of the size of Bronwyn's drawing room. Her dad was adding logs to the fire when they entered. Emma was anxious to see if he'd be smiling or frowning when he finally turned around to greet them. Her heart sank when her dad's lips were drawn tight, and his usual broad smile was missing.

Her mum gave him a kiss on the cheek, which made her dad smile. Her dad's eyes twinkled at the loving gesture. She had seen a similar twinkle in Christopher's gaze when he held her close.

Sinking to the floor, Emma curled her feet under her and waited for her parents to sit on the couch. Once they were seated, she looked to her mum and said, "I don't understand the reasoning for the council's requests. I don't want to leave London."

"Luv, we discussed this earlier. Ye're goin' to marry a bloomin' PORF." With watery eyes, her mum continued, "I've never struggled with being a council member until today. Choosin' wot was best for our organization over wot I want was not easy." Her mum reached out to cup Emma's face. "Ye're a smart, strong-willed girl. I'm ever so proud of ye."

Emma sat back, pulling away from her mum's touch. If she was so smart, why wasn't she able to figure out the logic in leaving her shop, her family, her friends; all for the unknown. Yes, she could set up shop in a new town, but the council's request precluded her from doing so by limiting her to designing for the stranger, Miss Suttingham. "Explain why Miss Suttingham's name was the only one on the list, then?"

"My, my. I can't believe Mr. Neale has shared that with ye."

Emma rarely saw her mum in a state of surprise. Was her mum's reaction due to Christopher having openly shared the information prior to their union or because he had informed her at all? He was a brilliant barrister, and he could have kept the details a secret if he wished. Happiness spread through her chest. Christopher trusted her, and he'd given her the option to stay or leave. As a husband, he'd have every right to order her to journey with him. Lifting her gaze to her parents, Emma replied. "He did. He said I could decide if I want to stay or go."

Her dad's lips finally broke into a smile. "See, luv, I told ye he wouldn't force her." He leaned back and wrapped an arm about his wife's shoulders. "He'll go get things done and come home to Em."

Rounding on her dad, her mum said, "That is not wot the council intended. We explained it all to him."

The subtle movements of give and take between her parents were intriguing. Emma hadn't paid close attention to her parents' actions before. But the gentle stroke of her dad's thumb, her mum's tendency to lean into her dad, struck Emma to the core. It was the same with her and Christopher. Her body sought to be closer to Christopher whenever he was near, and whenever possible, Christopher would gently caress her or provide soothing touches.

Her dad's booming, *"Ha!"* brought her attention back to her parents.

With a smirk, her dad said, "Then ye must have left somethin' out. Mr. Neale is a fine barrister—"

Her mum rounded on Emma. "Why would ye even consider letting yer husband leave ye behind?"

Emma snapped back, "Why would I leave my family? The Network needs me here."

Her mum sank back and leaned into Emma's dad. The woman Emma loved and admired most sat unmoving with a look of disappointment upon her delicate features. Recoiling on the inside, Emma admitted she'd been rude and disrespectful. "I'm sorry, Mum."

With a nod, her mum acknowledged her apology. "I'm not gonna say this again, so listen carefully, child. Ye marry Mr. Neale, ye become a PORF, and yer priorities and responsibilities change. The Network will support ye. Yer family will always be yer family. But yer future... well, only ye get to decide upon that. No one else, ye understand?"

Emma shook her head. She was stubborn. But as usual, her mum was right—her future was within her control. "Aye." Christopher was her future. She cared for the man deeply, more than she thought herself capable of. Just thinking of him eased some of the ache in her heart.

Her dad leaned forward and hauled Emma into his lap like she was five all over again. He had the same serious set to his features that he'd worn the day he asked Emma for her permission to marry her mum. "Girl, I've never known ye to back down from a challenge, and no matter wot ye decide, I'll support ye." He placed a kiss upon her forehead and then set Emma on her feet. "Ye want to walk back to yer shop or ride in a hack?"

Her dad hated cramped quarters. She gave him a smile and walked to the door. Hand on the latch, Emma said, "I fink I'll take a hack...alone. Simon and the boys will follow—no need for ye to be traipsing about town at this hour." She closed the door behind her, but not before she caught a glimpse at her dad's broad grin and her mum's sad but proud, watery eyes.

CHAPTER TWENTY-TWO

*A*ligning the sheets of parchment in his hands, Christopher tapped the bottoms to his desk. Four damn days of meetings and discussions with Lord Weathersbee and Landon had worn Christopher's patience thin. He hadn't managed to escape to spend a single moment with Emma. He'd tried to listen to the staff's whispers, but none gave Christopher any clue what had been preoccupying his betrothed's time. He had drafted a note explaining his absence, which had also included some rather intimate details of what he wanted and had been dreaming of doing with Emma, but thought better of sending it, knowing someone would have to read it to her. He'd thrown the love letter into the fire, and as it turned to ashes, so had Christopher's hopes of her accompanying him. Instead, he relayed messages to Emma via her guard, Simon, hoping Emma understood how time intensive it was to prepare for his departure.

Christopher froze at the rap at his office door.

"Enter." It was Simon. A breath trapped in his chest, Christopher waited for the man to approach.

Bent at the waist so Weathersbee and Landon wouldn't be able to hear, Simon said softly, "Mr. Neale, Miss Lennox wants ye to know she fully understands. *And* to let ye know she's too busy to keep responding to yer messages. She asks ye to stop sending me back and forth for no reason."

Christopher concentrated on relaxing every clenched muscle in his body. He calmly placed the papers flat upon the desk and turned to address Simon. "Tell Miss Lennox..."

"Mr. Neale, if ye don't mind, may I give ye some advice?"

The bold request had Christopher narrowing his gaze at the man.

Simon's Adam's apple bobbed. "Me mistress is no' lying. She's been running about faster than a hare. Don't ask me wot she's about cuz I don't know, and she ain't talkin' to no one. If ye want answers, ye best figure out a way to go see her yerself."

The fear that Emma would simply tell him to go to the New World alone had kept him hiding in his offices. He released a sigh. He could no longer avoid the discussion. "Please inform Miss Lennox to expect me later this eve."

The relief that washed over Simon's features was clear for all the men in the room to see. Simon nodded and rushed out of the office.

Weathersbee rose and tapped his knuckles on

Christopher's desk twice. "I believe I've accomplished all I wish for the day. I shall return tomorrow."

Christopher raised his eyes to the man, who was proving to be rather resourceful and extremely proficient at learning the operations of the office. In less than a week, Weathersbee had managed to set the employees at ease regarding Christopher's pending departure for an unspecified time period. They all believed Christopher to be planning an extravagantly romantic adventure for his bride.

Donning his coat, Weathersbee said, "Best wishes for your meeting this eve, Mr. Neale."

Landon, who had remained mute for most of their afternoon discussions, said, "Will you be attending Hereford's soiree tonight, Weathersbee?"

"Yes. I had planned on attending for a spell. At least long enough to garner any information that might assist us in Millard's case." Without waiting for a response, Weathersbee slid the last button into place and, with a curt nod, left Christopher's office.

Landon stood and moved to the window as Weathersbee walked out. His brother carefully shifted the drapes to the side. "I suspect the old man's motivations for attending this evening's entertainment is not solely linked to our case."

Christopher glanced up from the case file he'd opened. "What other reason could there be?"

"Did you know...Weathersbee's papa's estate was but a few miles away from our grandfather's?"

Rolling his head to one side, Christopher kneaded his

strained neck muscles. "What are you implying?" Landon was always suspicious of others' motivations, but his distrust had multiplied upon claiming his position as Head PORF.

"Mama was renowned for her beauty before Grandfather disowned her for marrying Papa." Landon's breath fogged the window. He cleared the glass pane with his sleeve and intently peered out again.

"And what does that have to do with Weathersbee?"

"Hmph." Landon let the curtain fall back into place and returned to his seat in front of Christopher. "I'm not sure, but the man's gaze lingers on Mama a moment too long for my liking."

What would it matter to Landon if Weathersbee was interested in their mama? A spark of ire at his brother's meddling spurred Christopher to ask, "Are you opposed to the idea of Mama finding love and remarrying?"

"You know I'm not. But Weathersbee? He's younger than Mama."

Christopher chuckled at Landon's appalled expression. "Brother, you are a stick in the mud. Mama is quite capable of taking care of herself. Now, promise to leave matters alone."

"I promised not to interfere with Weathersbee running the firm. I will not make the same promise regarding Mama." Landon shook his head and glared at Christopher.

Christopher was in no mood to debate the issue with his brother. "I'll leave it up to Mama to sort you out. I have many matters of my own to rectify."

"Like speaking to your betrothed about whatever issue has caused you to stay away from her for...well, too many days in my mind."

Irritated, Christopher barked, "Unless you have any wisdom to impart, I suggest you leave."

"Having married a former Network member myself, I shall impart my hard-won knowledge. The Network raises its girls to be strong and brave, but that doesn't mean they do not possess fears. I'm certain Emma shares the same concerns as you about the mission. My recommendation is you find a way to face them together." His brother unwound his long form and stood. "I shall keep an eye on Weathersbee since I presume you will be otherwise occupied this eve."

Christopher waved his brother off and returned to stare at the pages before him. He had let his fear of rejection rule him for days, preventing him from seeing the woman he loved. It was possible Emma, regardless if she loved him or not, would let her worries about leaving her family prevent her from agreeing to accompany him.

He would miss the birth of Landon and Bronwyn's firstborn. Drumming his fingers upon his desk, he waited for more depressing thoughts to come. Instead, images of Emma, pregnant and smiling, filled his mind. He reached into the breast pocket of his jacket and fingered the posy ring that had remained close to his heart. The ring should be settled upon Emma's finger. He'd rectify that tonight.

Reordering the files on his desk into alphabetical order, the question of what had kept Emma preoccupied for days kept poking at his mind. Rather than hypothesizing, he needed to go to her. The last folder remaining was the one that contained the carefully crafted list of Network members that he and Landon had selected to relocate to the New World. Christopher opened the file and examined the list once more. The decision upon which members to send to America had taken an extraordinary amount of time and a fair amount of consideration. Families would be disbanded, and several critical positions within PORF households would have to be filled. The long days and nights working alongside Landon were poignant reminders of how things used to be before Landon inherited the earldom. It also reinforced how much Christopher would miss his older brother's sound guidance.

The flicker of the candle reminded Christopher to check his pocket watch. Half-past eight—later than he had planned to leave, but Emma should still be awake. Raising his arms above his head, he stretched out his tired, sore back and then lowered his arms to roll his aching shoulders. The thought of seeing Emma refueled his lagging body. He grabbed the list of Network members, folded it precisely into quarters, and placed it alongside Emma's posy ring. Christopher's stomach growled. He would head home and have Cook prepare a picnic basket. Emma had a tendency to skip meals too. He smiled at the idea of sharing a repast with her again. He'd made it two blocks from the offices before a footman emerged from the shadows and began to follow him unusually close.

Swiveling to confront the guard, Christopher asked, "What is the matter?"

Simon replied, "Nuffin, sir. Miss Lennox asked that we made sure ye made it safe back to her shop, is all."

"Very well. We will make a quick detour to my town-house to pick up some food, and then we can be on our way."

Grinning like a fool, Simon revealed a picnic basket from behind his back. "Already done, sir."

Damnation, he'd had the notion mere moments ago; the Network could not have known his wishes. No, but they had anticipated them—meddling fools. But Christopher had to admit, in this instance, it was a good thing. Sometimes good intentions do result in favorable outcomes. It didn't make him sympathetic to their interfering ways, but he did appreciate their concern.

Striding across town, Christopher's nerves finally settled enough that he no longer felt nausea at the idea of asking Emma to leave her shop, family, and friends behind in return for an undefined future with him. Christopher mounted the steps to Emma's front door, resolved to obtain her answer. He took the food from Simon, who was still grinning, and pushed forward into Emma's shop. The bell tinkled overhead as the door swooshed open. Christopher scanned the shop. "Emma?"

"I'll be rit with ye." Emma's steady voice came from above.

"Has your dad arrived for the eve?"

Emma appeared on the steps in a lovely, light-blue

day dress. "He's come and gone. Lock me door and turn the sign."

He did as he was instructed and heard Emma sigh. Taking slow, methodical steps, he joined her on the stairs. "What is the matter?"

Hands on her hips, Emma asked, "Do ye always comply without hesitation?"

"Not always. I might object if there were a good reason to."

Emma frowned and turned to mount the steps. Following close behind, he noted the sagging of her normally taut straight shoulders. He froze as he reached the landing. Pillows had been arranged around a blanket on the floor.

Emma gracefully sank down on the far corner and curled her feet under her skirts. "Are ye goin' to join me or stand there starin'?"

Of course she knew of his plans. Nothing was kept secret amongst the Network. He placed the basket in the center of the blanket and sat with both legs stretched out in front, crossed at the ankles. "Simon tells me you've been extremely busy."

She raised her gaze to meet his. "Aye. All because of ye and yer bloomin' plans."

"My plans?"

"I'm not likin' the idea of ye marryin' me and then ye leavin'."

Christopher's heart burst with hope.

The angry slope of her brows told him she was

deadly serious when she said, "It's not the union I'd imagined when I agreed to wed ye."

Trying to control the mixture of fear and hope rioting through his veins, Christopher swallowed and then said, "Enlighten me. What type of union did you envision for us?"

Busy pulling out the food from the basket, Emma began mumbling, more to herself than answering his question. "It's not like I wanted a fancy life or anythin'. I was content." Emma paused, hand in midair with a shiny red apple. "Aye, I would have been happy if me life continued to go on the same but with a husband." Emma snorted—*Liar.* Catching herself, she handed him the apple and repeated, "I jus' didn't imagine being married and then separated from me husband."

"I had not pictured to be an ocean apart from my wife when I proposed. But I'll not force you to do anything against your will. I had assumed as part of the Network, you understood our lives would never be the same once we received the mark." He took the apple and bit deeply to prevent himself from speaking more.

"I do understand, and that's the reason why I've been bloomin' workin' day and night to prepare." Emma reached back into the basket and pulled out a roasted chicken leg.

Swallowing, Christopher asked hopefully, "Prepare to leave?"

Emma sat there, staring at him as she chewed the dark meat that she'd bitten off. It felt like a century before she finally patted her mouth with a napkin and said, "Aye."

He lurched forward. A great wave of energy forged through him. His forehead touched hers, and he kissed her smiling lips. "What made you decide to leave?"

"Hmm...let me see, it might have been yer dastardly kisses." Emma giggled as he kissed her again. Pulling back, his wife-to-be cupped his face and stared into his eyes. "I'm sorry, me noggin wasn't workin' right when ye first explained. I was confused and scared."

Christopher lowered his head again. This time he lingered, taking his time to kiss Emma until she relaxed against him. He wanted to reassure her, banish her worries. When she looped her arms about his neck, he relaxed into the kiss and savored the sweet taste of her mixed with the remaining tart juices of the apple.

His elbow hit the basket, and he remembered where they were. "Emma, I must tell you something."

She tilted her chin up. He couldn't resist. He bent and indulged in sultry open-mouth kisses until she was left breathless.

He ran his thumb over her furrowed brow. Emma said, "Now ye have me worried again."

"Emma Lennox, I've fallen in love with you."

"But ye hardly know me."

"That is the madness of it." He searched her eyes for understanding and then added, "I've never believed a person can fall in love with another upon sight. Yet, since the day I met you, I've not been able to think upon anyone else. At first,

I thought it was merely physical attraction, but that doesn't explain why it is your voice in my head challenging me to do better or why I want to seek out your opinion on everything."

She placed a hand over his heart, and the parchment crinkled. He sat up, pulling her with him. Christopher reached into his pocket and withdrew the list with the names of the Network contingent they were to escort. "And I'd dearly love your advice on the list of people Landon and I have devised."

Emma peered down as he unfolded the paper. Head bent, she asked, "Wot's it say?"

He pulled her closer and then pointed to the first column. "Their names,"—he shifted his finger to hover over the next column—"and these are the advantages and disadvantages we considered if they were to leave their present position."

Emma pointed to the top of the list. "'Tis me name. Why did ye fink I should go with ye?"

"Those reasons were developed by Landon, not I."

She tilted her head to look up at him. He couldn't resist kissing the frown from her brow. "I couldn't be objective. I desperately wanted you to come with me. I couldn't bear the thought of not waking up next to you every morn, but I didn't want to force you into something you would hate me for later."

"I love ye for giving me the time to figure it out on me own." Emma rested her head against his shoulder and released a sigh. "I'm looking forward to marrying ye, Christopher Neale, but I'm afraid once we wed, ye'll not be able to get rid of me. I've been told I'm rather stubborn, and I'll not be separated from me husband."

Reaching into his coat pocket once more, he extracted Emma's ring. Twirling the gold band until Emma could see the engraving, he said, "It says, *me kisses are fer ye*."

Emma stared at the posy ring and then raised her hand out for him. As he slid the ring on her finger, Emma pressed her mouth to his. She shifted. Her knees on either side of his hips, she straddled him and pushed her chest to his. She was so close he could feel her heart beating as wildly as his own. Christopher wrapped his arms around her waist. He was never letting go of this woman.

CHAPTER TWENTY-THREE

*F*irmly seated upon her betrothed's lap, entangled in his arms, Emma's entire world narrowed and centered upon one man—Christopher. Warm. Safe. Secure. Her worries about the future slipped from her mind. Undoubtedly, they would return later, but for now, she wanted to languish in the moment. Emma boldly pushed Christopher to lie on his back.

"Ow." His head had hit the floor.

Rolling forward, Emma placed her hands on either side of Christopher's head. She giggled and removed the half-eaten chicken leg that he had landed upon. "Sorry."

Taking the bone out of her hand, Christopher threw it back into the picnic basket. Face-to-face, Emma raised her hand and smoothed the worry lines creasing his forehead. Dark shadows sat beneath his playful brown eyes. "I can see ye have been working long hours." She cupped his face and ran her thumb over his cheekbone. He needed rest. He needed a wife to take care of him.

He turned and kissed her palm. "Requesting a member to give up the only life he or she has ever known is not something one does without significant consideration."

At the tender gesture, she lowered to capture the lips that had just branded her hand. Emma meant to lightly brush her lips over his, but when his fingers curled behind her head, she crushed herself to him until he was the one left breathless.

Shifting down his hard body, she rested her cheek on his shoulder and peered up at him. "Is that wot ye and Lord Hadfield have been discussin' behind closed doors for past few nights—the bloomin' list?"

His chest rumbled in her ear. "Landon will be your brother soon. He won't tolerate you referring to him as Lord Hadfield." His hand came to rest atop her head and then trailed down her neck and along her spine.

Emma snuggled closer. She'd always kept her distance from others, but she was drawn to Christopher and his caresses. It made her feel treasured. Emma drummed her fingers over his chest instead of working on sliding the three buttons of his jacket loose. "Ye didn't answer me question, luv."

Christopher's hand paused mid-stroke down her back. "I like it when you call me love."

"Then I shall continue—*if* ye answer me questions."

He chuckled and said, "Yes. I was gathering the names of the members to be selected for the assignment of supporting Lord Burke. I wanted Landon's insight, but in fact, for once in our lives, he proved as unfamiliar with the topic as I. So you see, my dear, it is *your* assistance I need."

His request wreaked all sorts of havoc on Emma. He wanted her opinion, which meant he valued her judgment. Emma flattened a hand upon his chest and pushed herself up to sit astride once again. She searched her soon to be husband's handsome features. Honest. Sincere. Christopher was not the complacent second son she had assumed him to be. "Ye need me?"

"Aye. There is no one else I trust."

A lump formed in her throat. Emma's finger traced the outline of one of his buttons. She let the wave of pleasure of being desired roll through her. Emma raised her gaze to his and said, "I've faith in ye too." She kissed him once more. The rub of his coat against her chest and the intensity of his gaze brought about both a physical and a more profound need within her. She wanted to reassure him he'd not misplaced his trust in her. Staring into his eyes, she shifted her hips lower. She wanted more than kisses. The craving to prove she was his and would be forever had her hips rotating until she felt his cock bulging against her core. Her dress slipped off her shoulders. Christopher had managed to release the ribbons of both her dress and stays and was skillfully divesting her of her clothing. Smiling at his talent, she rose slightly to pull her hands through the gaping sleeves, but in order to be free of the material, she had to pull back further from his warm body to shimmy out of her dress. The gleam of desire shone brightly in Christopher's eyes. Emboldened, Emma ran her fingers along the seam of his coat until they reached the top button.

Christopher inhaled sharply. "You, my dear, are eliciting every ungentlemanly thought I possess."

She eased the top button through its hole. "And ye are makin' me blood boil." She began to work on the second button.

Christopher emitted a low growl from the back of his throat.

She paused and lifted her gaze back to his eyes. "Is somethin' the matter, luv?"

His lips thinned into a straight line. Christopher slowly rolled his head from side to side. Emma freed the last button and spread his coat wide before running her hands up his sides and over his chest. The friction of the fine material against her palms sent shivers through her. "I fink it only fair I see ye naked before we wed."

She tugged on his waistcoat, urging him to sit up. Christopher complied, rolling to a sitting position, which shifted her hips, causing her center to graze against his manhood. The ache between her legs intensified, stalling her hand on his cravat.

"What will you do once you have me naked?" Christopher's voice deepened.

Emma grinned at his teasing remark. "Hmmm. Perhaps I'll lull ye to sleep, as ye did to me last time." Her bare skin pebbled at the memory of his hands kneading her muscles.

Emma slid the material from his neck as he removed his waistcoat, and together, they tugged his lawn shirt over his head. Emma didn't wait to run her hands over his shoulders and down his naked chest.

Christopher trailed light kisses along her neck and shoulder. "The thought of your hands roaming all over me isn't likely to induce my body to sleep."

Chest to chest, Emma delighted in the intimacy of being held close with no barriers between them. "Ye're still wearing yer breeches, and I want them off."

Effortlessly he lifted her by the waist and maneuvered her to sit next to him. While he did as she bid, she moved the heavy basket out of the way. Emma began to adjust the brightly colored pillows, but she froze. Christopher's smooth, creamy skin simply begged for her attention.

Intrigued, she skimmed her hand up over his torso that was adorned with a sprinkling of dark hair. He inhaled deeply and held his breath as she lowered her trembling hand back down to rest at his waist.

His gaze bored into her.

She ran her unsteady hand over his taut stomach. "Yer skin is hot."

"And I see you are cold." He trailed the back of his fingers along her arm. "Come, let me warm you."

Emma snuggled into his arms—he was her new haven. Christopher lowered them to lie upon the floor on their sides. She rested her head on his arm and closed her eyes. The brush of Christopher's warm breath upon her face set her cheeks aflame. She lay bare, ready to give herself over to the man she was to wed. His warm lips gently urged her mouth apart. She enjoyed his slow, tantalizing kisses. She wrapped her arm around his waist, palm flat against his back. Emma released his mouth merely long enough to whisper, "I love ye," before her tongue peeked out to tangle with Christopher's.

She raked her fingertips down his back, and every muscle of her future husband tensed. "I'm sorry—did I hurt ye?"

"Nothing to be sorry about...I'm a tad ticklish."

A giggle escaped her. "Ye're not serious, are ye?"

"Deadly."

"Are ye ticklish everywhere?" She lowered her hand to stroke his manhood that poked against her stomach.

A flicker of alarm flared in his gaze. "Not everywhere." A deep rumble escaped Christopher as she rubbed the tip of him with her thumb. He growled, "And that, my dear, will certainly not cause me to fall asleep."

She rolled slightly forward to kiss him once more. Her grip tightened about his cock as his warm hand circled her bottom.

Easing her onto her back, Christopher loomed over her. "Are you sure you want to marry me?"

Hoping to lighten the mood, she blew the wayward strands from her forehead and answered, "Aye, ye'll do."

He chuckled. "Perhaps I'll have to show you just how well I'll do."

Instead of kissing her again, he slowly ran a fingertip over her collar bone and then down the center of her body until he slipped a finger between her nether lips. He stroked until her eyes rolled back and a desire-filled moan escaped her. Christopher lingered, suckling on her breast and occasionally releasing her to flick his tongue over her nipple. Little bursts of light appeared behind her eyelids. Fingers continued to circle the sensitive nub at her core. Christopher shifted to place kisses down her middle. Emma's eyes popped open. He spread her legs wider to accommodate his shoulders. Poised over her, Christopher bent and gave her the most intimate kiss possible. His tongue slid along her nether lips.

Emma arched her back. "Chris... Christopher!"

The tip of his tongue circled the aching bud, mimicking his earlier motions with his fingers. She reached down to grasp his shoulder, but her hand landed on the back of his head, and she tugged on his hair.

He lifted his head and said, "We should stop." Christopher shifted and rolled to her side. "We should wait until after we have said our vows."

Eyes fluttering open, she glared at her husband-to-be. "Do ye love me?"

"Aye, with all my heart."

"And I love ye." She tugged him over her again. Bringing his head down to hers, she whispered, "I want ye."

His gaze roamed over her face. She met his stare. Whatever he'd been searching for, he must have found it, for he positioned himself between her legs and ready to enter her. "I love you, Emma."

Before she could reply, she bit down on her bottom lip, stifling a cry of surprise as he filled her completely. Their bodies, joined intimately, created a bond within Emma that was stronger than anything she'd ever experienced. When he moved slowly in and out of her, she dug her fingers into his bottom. In the few instances she'd spied couples mating, the man had been far more vigorous. Her inner muscles began to clench. Christopher deepened his thrusts but maintained a rhythmic pace. Emma's heart pounded hard against her chest. She lifted her hips to meet his over and over. Her muscles spasmed, and the twinkling lights returned beneath her eyelids. Christopher grunted as he entered her one last time before a warmth radiated through her core, sending her into depths of bliss she'd never known.

Muscles quivering, Christopher fell on top of her, bracing his weight upon his forearms. "I was wrong. You have induced my body to seek out slumber."

He rolled aside, facing her. Draping a leg over his, Emma settled herself next to him and closed her eyes, ignoring the pang of hunger. She was too exhausted to eat. The food would have to wait until later.

CHAPTER TWENTY-FOUR

*E*mma wrapped her frayed coverlet tighter about her, tucking a corner in the valley between her breasts. She peered over at Christopher's sleeping form, covered with one of the cotton sheets from her bed. He slept on his side, hand tucked beneath the bright-yellow silk pillow under his head. His dark mane was disheveled —no doubt from her fingers threading and pulling on his hair. A buoyant joy placed a bounce in her step as she crept on the balls of her feet to retrieve the parchment that lay next to the abandoned picnic basket. Carefully picking up the folded paper, she tiptoed to the window. Shifting the curtains aside to let in what little moonlight was left, Emma unfolded the list of Network members that were to journey with them. Squinting at the neat, bold letters, Emma sounded out the names but could not make out the other words on the paper. Bah. If she was to become a bloomin' PORF, she'd have to learn to read.

She jumped as Christopher placed a kiss upon her bare shoulder. "Ye did a fine job."

"My thanks. I had hoped you would approve of those on the list."

Emma turned to wrap her arms around his waist. He was garbed in only his breeches. Resting her cheek against him, she said, "While we journey to the New World, will ye teach me how to read?"

"If you wish me to, yes. But now that you are accompanying me, there is no need."

Emma placed a quick kiss on his chest. "Ye're sweet to say that, but I'll be needin' to know how to read and write if I'm to succeed as a PORF."

His relaxed features transformed into a scowl. "I don't want you to change. I love you just as you are."

"We will both need to change after we wed and receive the mark of a PORF." Happy to see Christopher smile at her response, Emma continued, "And the good thing is we get to do it together."

He bent to kiss her, and she rose up to meet him halfway. Instead of a long, drugging kiss Emma hoped to receive, Christopher broke away and slipped his arm beneath her knees. He carried her over to her bed and gently laid her down. Christopher surprised her again by not joining her. Instead, he left her and went into the loft. Emma beamed a smile at the rattle of plates. He was going to bring her food. She sighed—how lucky she was to marry a thoughtful man.

Arms loaded with plates piled with food, Christopher

asked, "Would you mind reviewing the list in detail with me later this eve?"

"We can't this eve. We are to attend Bronwyn's ball."

With a stubborn jut of his chin, Christopher suggested, "After the ball then."

The temptation to spend another night with Christopher was too great. She nodded and said, "I sorted out the names, but I couldn't read yer reasoning."

Emma took the offered plate of cheese and bread. Christopher pinched the roll of bread she'd been eyeing. He took a bite and then offered it to her. She wasn't sure if she was angry or happy at his actions. "Are ye going to take half the cheese as well?"

He shook his head and winked at her as he left once more. Emma's attention remained fixed on his backside as he strode away. He had a fine bottom with cheeks that filled her hands. She flopped back onto the bed and closed her eyes. Memories of him filling her had her hips wiggling. Her eyes popped back open as his warm breath brushed against the tops of her breasts. Christopher loomed over her holding out a wedge of cheese. Disappointed to see he had donned his lawn shirt, she frowned at his offering.

Arching a brow, Christopher asked, "Is the cheese not to your liking? Or were you wanting something else?"

She grabbed the cheese and lowered her gaze, and his manhood twitched in his breeches. She wasn't the only one remembering the events of the previous night. Licking her lips, she took a bite. Christopher's chuckle turned into a groan.

"You are pure temptation." Christopher dodged behind the screen that formed her makeshift dressing room. "Is this fine mint-green colored gown the glorious creation you will be wearing to Bronwyn's ball?"

He must be referring to the exquisite dress she had created for Arabelle.

"Nay. I shall be daring in a red gown with—"

Emma's words caught in her throat. Christopher reappeared, shirt tucked into his breeches, highlighting his trim waist. His hair finger-combed back into place, and a smile that could warm an entire room.

Standing before her with his hands behind his back, Christopher said, "It would be an honor if you allowed me to escort you to the ball."

She shook her head. "Bronwyn has requested I arrive early, along with Theo and your mama." The coverlet slipped down, exposing the tops of her nipples.

"Four Hadfield women gathered together," Christopher croaked out before his eyes fell to her chest as she grappled with the material to cover up her breasts. He grabbed his lawn shirt and pulled it over his head.

Emma scooted back to make room for him on the bed. "I'm not a Hadfield yet."

"Yet. But after last night..." He pulled her into his arms. "You're mine forever."

She had wished and dreamed of a devoted husband like her dad. Christopher was as caring and protective of his family as the man who had raised her.

Her dad. Blast! He had mentioned he'd check in on her in the morn.

The Neale household staff would have already noticed he'd not returned last night. Arghh... she was going to get an earful.

Pushing at Christopher's shoulders, Emma said, "Ye've got to leave. Me dad will be here soon."

"I'll stay with you until he arrives."

"No, ye will not. Now off with ye." Contrary to her words, Emma tilted her head as he lightly grazed the base of her neck with his teeth.

Christopher kissed his way up to her ear. "He won't be pleased to know I've remained the night."

"I'll... I'll handle him." She moaned as he took her earlobe between his lips.

Releasing her, he whispered, "What if I want to?"

"Owya. To be wed to a barrister." She shoved him back until they were eye to eye. "Are ye always goin' to argue with me?"

Christopher gave her a brief kiss and said, "Not always."

He slid from the bed and returned with a pink day dress. Hauled to her feet, she had no choice but to drop the coverlet to dress. Christopher's hands immediately went to her hips, bringing her an inch closer. His warm breath brushed over her breasts, pebbling her nipples. She wanted him to trail kisses over her chest like he had before. Her husband-to-be bent his head, took her nipple into his mouth, and suckled.

"Are ye trying to get killed?" She moaned her delight but kept her hands clenched at her sides. She looked at the faint stream of sunlight peeking through the curtains. "Me dad will be on his way."

With one last swirl of his tongue, Christopher straightened and placed a chaste kiss upon her forehead. "Promise you'll wait up for me after the ball."

Grabbing the dress from his hands, Emma nodded. "Ye better not make me wait long." Forgoing her stays, she leaned forward, brushing the tips of her nipples across his bare skin as she turned around and pulled the dress over her head. With her back to him, she slightly bent at the hips to shake out her skirts. Her bum brushed up against his erect manhood. Christopher sucked in a breath. But instead of reaching around to fondle her breasts like Emma wished he'd do, Christopher did the gentlemanly thing and helped her with the buttons at the back of her dress. It was nice to have help and not pull a muscle twisting and turning about. "Are ye nearly done?"

"Damnation, woman, stay still." Christopher's nimble fingers had excelled at releasing buttons, but he wasn't as adept at playing the maid. He released a sigh and said, "Done." Christopher hadn't even finished saying the word when the pounding at the front door started. Stepping around Emma, Christopher headed for the stairs. Trailing right behind him, Emma avoided tripping over skirts as she tried to match his long strides.

Blast. He reached the front door first. Swinging the door open, Christopher let her dad into the shop. "Good morning, Mr. Lennox."

"Humph. Was her mum not clear? No more night-time visits."

"I apologize. Mrs. Lennox was clear in her wishes."

Her dad entered and shoved Christopher out. "I need a word with Emma...in private." He shut the door and fastened the locks. "Ye two figure matters out?"

She wasn't exactly sure what her dad was referring to, but she and Christopher were in accord. Emma said, "Aye."

"Good. Did he share with ye the names of those he's chosen to go abroad?

Emma squinted at her dad to hide her shock. Her dad wasn't going to lecture her on having a gentleman stay overnight under her roof, and she wasn't going to prompt him. "Aye. I know who's to go."

"Well..."

"That's not for me to share. He's asked for me opinion, but we haven't had time to go over them all."

Her dad's beefy hands clenched, and his knuckles popped. "No time, huh."

There was a light rap at the front door. Her dad peered out the window and mumbled, "It's yer stubborn niece." He released the locks.

The door flew open, and Lady Arabelle waltzed past Mr. Lennox, who crept out the front door and left without a goodbye.

"Where did your father disappear to?" Lady Arabelle asked as she removed her gloves.

"He's off to work." Emma went up the stairs to retrieve Arabelle's gown. "Yer dress is ready. I'll jus' go box it up for ye."

Arabelle followed her up to the loft.

Reaching over Emma's shoulder, Arabelle pulled out the red gown. "You devil. Don't tell me you plan on wearing this ruby creation." She pressed the garment against her chest and twirled about. It absolutely divine." The mischievous twinkle in her eye shone brightly. Emma braced herself for Arabelle's request. "Let's switch gowns. You wear the green, and I get to wear the red."

Recalling how Christopher's voice had deepened earlier while in her closet, Emma considered the outrageous request. She wanted to incite that devilish gleam in his eyes when he was just about to kiss her.

Emma nodded. "Very well." Taking the red gown from Arabelle's grasp, she boxed it up and trudged down the stairs.

Emma waited by the door for Arabelle to descend.

Taking the box from Emma, Arabelle asked, "Do you always dine on the floor?" Arabelle shifted her gaze back to the stairs.

Ignoring the question, Emma said, "Have yer maid press the gown." She gently shoved Arabelle out the door. "I shall see ye at the ball."

Leaning back against the door, she slid the bolts into place. She needed to make a few quick alterations to the green dress. Alterations that would tempt her dear betrothed.

CHAPTER TWENTY-FIVE

$\mathcal{H}$aving never given his height much consideration prior, Christopher was newly thankful he had been blessed with a few extra inches as he scanned the crowd filling Landon's townhouse. Where was Emma? He scrutinized every darn woman dressed in red. He studied the throng of ladies that consisted of the usual set of debutantes and a few country misses, but there was no sign of his fiancée anywhere.

Landon murmured, "Did the council grant your request?"

He inwardly winced, recalling his earlier meeting with the Network elders. His anxiety level had risen prior to presenting his request to the council, but not as high as it was now. He'd sought approval of his plan to have one of them accompany him as he extended invitations to each Network member on his list personally. Christopher wanted each member to know that it was an offer, not a demand, and that they may choose to decline if they wished. That he remained unmarked worked to his advantage. He wanted the members to go willingly.

Christopher glanced at his brother. Landon had adopted a relaxed stance, but his eyes were filled with worry. "I did. Cadby and I are to begin visiting the families tomorrow." Landon's eyes narrowed at the mention of his father-in-law, but Christopher ignored his older brother's glare and nodded as more guests were announced. All the ceremonious aplomb grated on Christopher's nerves. He took a step back and waited while Landon smiled and formally greeted the guests. Onlookers would have thought the Earl of Hadfield was thoroughly enjoying the nonsensical idle chatter, but Christopher noticed the back of Landon's coat stretched taut. His brother's muscles grew tenser the longer the couple nattered on. Christopher scanned the room once more. With each passing second of not locating Emma, his pulse accelerated.

Having completed his salutations, Landon turned and asked, "How long do you anticipate it will take for you to obtain everyone's consent?"

"Cadby anticipates a week; I'd say a few days."

"Hmph. The man is not one to exaggerate." There was no love lost between Landon and his father-in-law, but his brother did respect the man.

"Aye, but I'm not one to dally." A honey blonde in a green dress, similar to the one he saw at Emma's shop, appeared briefly and exited onto the terrace. His heart leaped, but Emma had said she would be in red. His gaze flickered to Landon. "Have you seen my fiancée?"

"She's most likely with my wife. I was tied up at the Foreign Office this afternoon, and I haven't had a chance to locate Bronwyn." Landon's relaxed features remained in place, but his voice was definitely strained. "I had expected my wife to be here, next to me, greeting the piranhas...beg pardon, the guests."

Christopher smothered a laugh. "I'll leave you to your host duties. I'm off to find the women."

Leaving his brother's side, Christopher kept to the fringes of the crush. He milled about, relying on his ability to sense when she was near. The mass of bodies shifted like a school of fish. If the number of attendees determined the success of a ball, then Bronwyn's first official event as a host was a smashing victory.

Christopher spied his cousin Theo in the corner with her usual guards, Waterford and his wife, Lady Mary, and made his way towards the trio.

He greeted Theo with a quick peck on the cheek. "Have you seen Emma?" Christopher took a half step back.

His cousin, who was more like a sister, stared at him through narrowed eyes and replied, "Not recently." Theo's pleasant smile masked her displeasure.

It was never a good thing to be in Theo's bad graces. Christopher asked, "Why are you angry at me?"

The woman's lips thinned into a straight line briefly. When he raised an eyebrow, Theo answered, "Your fiancée is the best modiste in town, and you are stealing her away."

Ah. Given the request for them to venture off was from the Network and not a PORF dictate, it had obviously upset his cousin. The interference of either group affected many. Mayhap both parties would soon learn that meddling, no matter how well intended, had significant consequences.

Lowering his voice, Christopher said, "As you are aware, one decision can have an impact that trickles down to a countless number of souls." With his private message delivered, Christopher smiled at the small group and settled his attention upon Theo. "Sarah and Maude will ensure your gowns will be as magnificent as the one you are wearing this eve."

Theo replied, "Hmph. Not surprised it would take two to replace Emma."

His cousin was right. The loss of Emma to both the Network and PORFs would be great. Selfish as it may be, he wasn't going to be separated from Emma—ever.

Christopher spun and followed Waterford's intense gaze. Bronwyn and his mama stood on either side of Landon. Uncertain when or if he'd see them again, he placed a hand over his chest to ease the sharp, hot stab to his heart. He was leaving them, his family, to start anew with Emma. Melancholy transformed into panic. Where in the blazes was Emma?

Theo placed a hand on his arm. She must have sensed his unease. "There is nothing to worry about. Emma is well guarded and protected here tonight."

Her comment further rattled his nerves. Once they were abroad with only a small contingent of Network members, who would assist him in ensuring Emma's safety? The New World was reputed to be wild and dangerous. Damnation. Unlike Landon, he often hastily agreed to matters. But this wasn't a matter of haste; he wanted Emma, and he was confident she was the woman for him.

Christopher rolled slightly onto the balls of his feet to gain a few more inches over the sea of coiffeurs. "Still, I won't be sure until I have her within sight at the very least."

"Go find her...you are worse than Landon." Theo turned him by the arm and gave him a slight shove in the direction of the gardens.

Emma wouldn't have risked leaving the crowd without an escort. Except the glimpse of a red gown out on the terrace proved Theo was right. The woman disappeared down the stairs that led to the darkened gardens. Emma had mentioned something about assisting Hereford.

Marching towards the exit, Christopher halted midstride when Hereford appeared at his side.

Eyebrows furrowed, Hereford asked, "Have you seen Emma or Arabelle?" The man was impeccably dressed, but his whole countenance radiated agitation.

"No. I've not seen either of them." Christopher grasped Hereford's upper arm, attempting to sidestep, but they both moved in the same direction.

"Grr. Those two are going to be the death of me."

Hereford looked over Christopher's shoulder and searched the crowd. "They wandered off together. Lord knows what the pair are up to."

Facing the terrace doors, Christopher said, "I'll search the gardens. You continue the search indoors."

Hereford nodded and headed, grumbling, into the throng of guests.

Slipping through the doors into the brisk night air, Christopher made his way to the set of stairs the woman in red had taken. At the bottom, he followed his instincts and searched the hedges. A sliver of shimmering mint-green silk caught his attention. Moving as stealthily as he could along the pebbled path, Christopher held his breath.

A small hand reached out, and fingers dug into his upper arm. His assailant tugged him into the prickly shrubbery. He wrapped his fingers about the cold, gloved hand that covered his mouth.

"Ow."

He released his fiancée and swiveled to face her. "Emma! What the devil?"

"Shh!" Emma's eyes slid to a couple a few feet away.

A woman in a daring ruby silk gown smiled down at a gentleman on one knee. Their features were too shadowed to identify.

Christopher reached for Emma's hand and pressed his lips against her wrist. Damn the material that created a barrier between them. Emma withdrew her hand and frowned up at him. Momentarily distracted by the blaze within his beautiful fiancée's eyes, Christopher brushed his mouth over her lips. Emma opened for him and returned his kisses. He tried to draw her closer, but she pushed against his chest. "Ye stop that, or we'll not be returning to the ball."

He turned Emma by the shoulders to face the couple. "Is that Arabelle and Markinson?"

"Aye. And ye need not interfere." She looked over her shoulder and added, "Markinson jus' needed time and for everyone to stop pokin' about his business. Men can be contrary, ye know. The more ye push them one way, the more likely they'll run the other. Now, shh. Let's see how Arabelle handles him."

"With care, I hope."

Emma giggled. "He's no pansy. He'll do fine."

Markinson pulled his hand from his pocket, extending a rather large diamond that glittered in the moonlight. Except Arabelle had both hands firmly clasped behind her back and shook her head. The droop of the man's shoulders meant only one thing. Arabelle had refused. What game was Arabelle playing? This is what she had wished for, for over a year. Christopher's hands left Emma's shoulders, and he shifted forward.

Emma hauled him back before he revealed them both. In a harsh whisper, Emma asked, "Wot are ye doin'?"

"I'm going to put an end to this nonsense."

She tilted her head, exposing her tantalizing neck. Christopher froze. Emma said, "Weren't ye the one goin' on about how everyone should have the ability to choose their own future?"

"I was referring to the members of the Network...not the rake about to ruin a family member."

Emma placed a chaste kiss upon his cheek. "I love ye for being protective over me niece, but if ye go bargin' through the gardens, Markinson will have no choice. And Arabelle will forever believe he married her only to prevent a scandal or some such nonsense." With a sigh, Emma continued, "We need to give them the time and space to sort it all out. Now, keep a lookout for one of these nosy matrons of the ton I hear about."

Her kiss subdued his anger. Christopher listened to the wisdom of his soon-to-be wife and settled his hands about her waist. While Emma focused on the couple who stood entranced with each other, ignorant of the world about them, Christopher's attention was drawn to the delightful heart-shaped décolleté of Emma's gown.

He leaned down to nibble on his sweet fiancée's delectable little earlobe, but her pointy elbow hit him against the ribs. "Ouch." He straightened and rubbed the spot that Emma had injured.

The moon illuminated Arabelle, who was presently engulfed in Markinson's arms. The couple appeared to be guaranteeing their engagement with an energetic kiss.

"Wot are ye waiting for?" Emma asked, glaring up at him.

"You said not to meddle."

"Don't be daft. Ye can't let him muss up her hair." She turned and stepped closer, placing her hand flat over his heart. "Bring her back here, so I can escort her back to her brother and we can leave."

She slid her hand up and threaded her fingers through the hair at the back of his neck. He bent slightly, and the minx darted her tongue out to trace his bottom lip. Heat radiated through him. She boldly kissed him and mussed up his hair. Heart pounding in his ears, he released her lips but held her close. She grounded him. Emma winked, spun him around, and with a slight shove, she sent him spiraling towards Markinson.

He naturally detested being ordered about, but he didn't mind the idea of Emma bossing him about so long as he was granted boons like that last kiss. Walking with purpose, Christopher approached the couple, ready to be done with the evening. The sooner he had Emma alone, the better.

CHAPTER TWENTY-SIX

*T*wo weeks after the ball, Emma was more frustrated than satisfied with her engagement to Christopher. Sneaking about and arranging clandestine meetings wore on Emma's patience, yet it brought to light how exhilarating her future would be with Christopher. Leaning back against the solid wood door of his chambers, Emma waited for the pounding of her heart to slow.

Each night, her skills in going about undetected were challenged. She suspected the Network was aware of their nightly escapades. The change of guard times had altered at least twice a week for the past fortnight. She wasn't sure if the variation in times had been due to her unsanctioned activities with Christopher or the shifting of personnel. Christopher had quickly and meticulously gained the consent of every Network member on the list, allowing Landon and the Network elders to work together to reestablish a new sense of order. Her mum had shared that others had heard of Christopher's offers and were intrigued at the prospect of a new life abroad. Many had approached the council seeking approval to join the ranks of those to make the six-week journey across the sea. When members had been asked why they wished to relocate, all had stated they wished to give their support to Christopher, who would officially become a PORF tomorrow. A burst of pride invaded her heart—she couldn't wait to wed the man who was destined to be a great PORF. Her stomach cramped. She needed to discuss the details of what was to occur after their wedding ceremony tomorrow.

Squinting towards the bed, Emma whispered, "Christopher." Where was her bloomin' husband-to-be? With no moonlight, the room was darker than a cave. The door pushed against her, sending her stumbling forward.

"Sorry, love." Christopher, still on the other side of the door, whispered, "I brought us a late-night snack. I heard you skipped supper again."

She opened the door wider to allow Christopher in. "Ye didn't hear any such nonsense."

"Have you eaten?" The clatter of silverware against wood told Emma he was next to her.

"Nay. But no one told ye I hadn't, ye're jus' guessin'." She planted her hands on her hips, hoping she wouldn't topple over the tray that was most likely piled high with breads and sweets.

His warm breath brushed her check. "Come along before I get distracted."

She followed his soft footsteps and froze when he stopped. Waiting for Christopher to deposit the tray upon the bed, Emma counted out the four steps to the right that should place her in front of the window to draw back the thick double-layered curtain that kept the cold out. The dim rays of moonlight filtered through the gap and Emma turned to see the extravagant spread of food upon the bed.

"Did ye bring up the whole larder?"

Christopher chuckled. "I like to be prepared." He patted the space next to him.

She raised a knee to crawl up onto the luxurious bed that she had quickly become accustomed to sleeping in. Although she hardly slept. Most nights, by the time they finished detailing their long days combined with Christopher's love making, they had only a few hours until sunrise. Carefully balancing her weight so as not to topple any of the food about, she settled upon the mattress. Instead of sitting opposite her, Christopher slid in behind her and began his nightly ritual of kneading away the knots in her shoulders.

All the stress of creeping about was worth the bliss of Christopher's magical touch. His clever fingers and clever banter made her relax even when they discussed Network matters. Each night she'd wanted to broach the topic of the possibility of them never seeing family again. But fear of the answer kept her silent.

"Pet. Are you ready to tell me what has you in knots each eve?" His thumb grazed down her neck. "I work tirelessly each night to ease them, but if you do not share with me the cause, how am I to help prevent them?"

On a strangled breath she finally asked, "Will we see our families again?"

"That is my hope." His voice was filled with as much worry and pain as she felt having asked the question.

"I shall miss Sunday dinner with the Cadbys and Wednesday dinners with me own family." She twisted to face him and blinked back tears. "Today yer mama paid me a visit. She asked me to call her Mama..." The request had pierced her heart, since from the day they met, Aunt Henri had been like a second mum. Emma paused to swallow the large lump that choked her words. "I understand the need to support Lord Burke but..." She turned away and wiped her eyes with the back of her hand.

He pressed a soft kiss upon her shoulder. "Not only Lord Burke, but also you and I as we too will be PORFs after tomorrow. Some, not all, of the Network contingent have expressed specifically that they wish to serve us. If we return, they too will return. Likewise, if we decide to stay, they will too."

Emma leaned back against Christopher's solid chest as he wrapped his arms securely about her waist. She let her weary head fall back to rest. "Me brain is ready to become a PORF, but me heart..."

"I share your worries, my love." He didn't try to distract her with kisses but gave her a reassuring squeeze. "I've always had the wise counsel of my mama and Landon. I fear I shall fail without them. To oversee such a large number of Network members who have chosen to place their lives, trust their futures—"

Emma interrupted, "To you. They believe in ye like I do. Ye're strong, intelligent, and ye rule with a fair hand. A man worthy of following."

"I love you, Emma Lennox, for saying so, but I'm certain they have pledged their loyalty to us due to their faith in you." Cheek to cheek with Emma, he continued, "It's my hope to strengthen existing bonds and forge new ones. And as for family...well, there is the possibility we have already begun to increase the size of our own family." He rubbed her tummy. "And if we haven't, I'm willing to..."

As his words comforted her and eased some of her worry, she wanted to express how much she loved and needed him. She shifted to straddle him so she could speak face-to-face. "Luv, it would be an honor to carry yer babe." She plastered herself to him, kissing him until he rolled back and they were tangled amongst the covers. Her back bumped the tray. It was likely he hadn't eaten supper either. She extracted herself from his arms. Scooting back, she placed the tray between them. "I need to eat if I'm to keep up with ye tonight."

CHRISTOPHER EYED THE ELDERBERRY TART. Ever since his papa had advised the raw berries were potentially lethal, he never dared risk eating the fruit even when cooked. But they were Emma's favorite and he trusted

Cook wouldn't dare poison her. Still, he was wary as she raised the treat to her mouth. Forcing himself not to knock it from her hands, he busied himself placing a slice of cheese upon some bread.

The tip of Emma's tongue ran over her bottom lip, sweeping small crumbs into her mouth. He cleared his throat and said, "Do you have any concerns regarding our upcoming nuptials?"

She popped the rest of the tart in her mouth and moved to place the tray on the floor. Standing before him, she grinned and turned. He worked on releasing the row of buttons and untying the ribbons of her stays. The minx wiggled and let her dress drop to the floor. Naked, she slowly turned about and crawled back onto the bed, but instead of in front of him like before, she seated herself behind him. Her warm hands at his waist pulled his shirt loose and then over his head. The white material flew over his head and the garment landed on the edge of the bed. Emma began to rub the knots from his shoulders, but while her touch was intended to soothe, it only provoked his muscles to tense in anticipation of having her.

Emma's hands stilled. "Where will ye ask Cadby to place the mark?"

"Hmm...I've not yet decided. You?"

She wrapped her leg about his waist and lifted her foot. "Me ankle, like yer cousin Theo."

He grabbed her foot and began to rub the sole. Emma released a moan that had his cock twitching in his breeches. As her hands skimmed over his shoulder, he lifted his hand to trap hers. "Do you have a suggestion or are you simply trying to distract me?"

"I'm sharin' me worries as ye've asked. I've heard how much it bloody hurts to receive the mark." Emma tugged her hand free and began to massage his neck and then rubbed his aching temples. In a short span of a fortnight, the woman had discovered all the spots he stored his stress.

"I can't believe *I'll* be a bloomin' PORF—*me*. I know how to aid and protect PORFs, but to be one...well, ye're gonna have to be patient with me."

Christopher chuckled. "You have more knowledge than I." Her breasts pushed up against his back as she stiffened.

"But it's in yer blood. It's yer fate as a Hadfield." Emma guided him to face her. "Have ye spoken with Lady Mary of late?"

"No. Why do you ask?"

"She came to pick up an order today. And she was mumbling to another—mind you I couldn't see anyone else about—stating her belief that one was not solely bound by fate. That we all get to choose our mate in life. Whoever she was talking to disagreed."

"What do you believe?"

She wrapped her arms around him at the waist. "I've always considered Lady Mary an odd duck, but a kind one. But I agree with the lady. I chose you."

"And I'm exceptionally fortunate that you did." He looked over his shoulder at her. "However, I distinctly recall the bizarre feeling that struck me, all the way through to my soul, the day you rushed past me on my brother's stairs. It was as if I'd only been existing and not living. After that moment, I was consumed by thoughts of you. I wanted you like no one else before. I have wondered why I had not met you before. Why now? Regardless, I can't imagine my life without you. I'm excited for our future."

Her hand lowered and his body immediately reacted to her touch. Oh, the woman definitely got him excited.

"What are ye most looking forward to?" She released the buttons of his falls and his cock sprang free. With a wicked grin, she wrapped her hand firmly about him and began to slowly stroke him from tip to base, her movements producing a small bead of liquid at the tip.

"Spending every day and eve with you." He pushed down his breeches until he was free of them. He spun around to face Emma. "Are you ready to marry me, Miss Emma Lennox?"

"Aye, but I might want ye to show me once more how ye plan to occupy me days and nights."

"As you wish. Lie on your stomach for me."

Without argument, she lay out flat. He placed his hands on her plump bottom. Oh how he loved the feel of the soft mounds in his hands. Giving each cheek a quick squeeze, he straddled her and settled his manhood to rest at her wet entrance. Leaning forward, he ran his hands over her bottom and then up her back. He trailed his fingertips along her sides until they touched her breasts and slowly kneaded his way back down. Emma released a moan of pleasure. He loved the way her body reacted to his touch. Repeating the motions, he slid forward slightly, his cock pressing closer to her core. He needed to bury himself inside her.

"Love, lift up onto your elbows for me." He guided her hips up and she rose to her knees. He entered her slowly. Tight from his impatience, he circled his hips, urging her inner muscles to loosen.

Emma's forehead dropped to the bed, the motion forcing him deeper. He wanted to go slow, but his body and Emma were not cooperating. The woman challenged his every movement. The slower he moved, the faster and more demanding she became. He wanted to wait to find his release, but the sensations mounted with each thrust. Emma's sighs of pleasure turned into deep moans of ecstasy. Grabbing her hips, he pulled her to him, hard and deep. His release pulsed throughout his body, leaving him lightheaded and winded. He collapsed to the bed. His muscles flexed as her hand skimmed his skin that was covered in a light sheen of sweat.

"Are ye no longer ticklish?"

"Love, you've milked me of every ounce of energy. I can't move, despite your devilish attempts to tickle me." He rolled over and pulled her atop of him.

Grinning down at him, she cupped his face. "Don't ye worry, I'll take care of ye." Her lips were upon his—soft and teasing. Then she replicated his own habit of trailing kisses along the collar bone. She didn't stop there. She kissed her way down the center of his body until she was able to take him into her mouth. The woman basked in the power to reinvigorate his manhood. The slightest touch from her and he was at the ready to pleasure her. When her lips were wrapped about his cock, it hardened with astonishing quickness given his recent release. The tip of him hit the palate of her mouth, yet she shifted and took him deeper. She was going to be the death of him, relentless in her pursuit to make him climax once more—but not before he brought her to her own first.

EPILOGUE

*C*hristopher rubbed his wife's back as she retched and heaved over the side of the *Quarter Moon.* He'd hoped the fresh air would help ease Emma's discomfort, but nothing had alleviated her nausea since they set foot upon the ship three weeks ago.

Captain Bane cautiously approached. "Mr. Neale, may I have a word?"

Emma waved him away. The journey to date had been devoid of pirate attacks. He scanned the ocean. Nothing but rolling swells. Not even a gleam of a storm brewing. "What is it, Captain?"

"If I have your permission to slow our speed, it might only extend our voyage a day or two, but the ship would sail smoother and perhaps Mrs. Neale would have an easier time aboard."

Christopher was considering the captain's suggestion when Emma stepped between them. At her full height, the top of Emma's head barely came level with the man's shoulders. Christopher grinned at the stubborn set of his wife's chin.

With all the poise of a queen, Emma said, "It's not the rollin' of the ship, Captain Bane, that has me ill. And I'll not hear of subjectin' everyone to a longer journey."

"As you wish, madame." Red faced, the captain bowed and took his leave.

Emma whirled about and poked Christopher in the chest. "'Tis all yer fault."

His pectoral muscles flexed at his wife's prodding. "How am I to blame?" He stepped closer to wrap his arms about her waist.

"Ye're too bloomin' tempting to resist." Emma grazed her hands up his chest around his neck. "Mayhap we should have waited until after our weddin' to begin a family."

"Emma Lennox Neale, you are the one who tempted me." He kissed her forehead and unwrapped her arms to turn her about to look out to sea. "Three more weeks, and we should be ashore." The moonlight glistened off the waves. Widening his stance, he drew her back, and she sagged against his chest. She was exhausted, but the tension in her body remained absent since the day of their wedding.

Emma sighed and rested her head back against his shoulder. "Goin' by me mum's pregnancies, that's about when this queasiness should end."

"Are you ready for what is to come?"

"I don't miss strainin' me eyes late at night and sortin'

bloomin' buttons. But I've been finkin' about our mission. Do ye fink Lord Burke will want our aid?"

Christopher chuckled. "I highly doubt it. We will be a reminder of what he left behind—a tainted title, duties to the Crown, and a desolate estate." He rubbed her arms to ward off the chill of the sea breeze. "However, if we succeed in executing my plan, he might come to understand we've come to help and not impede his goals."

"From all reports, this Eliza woman is rather determined to remain unattached, and not one to trust strangers easily."

"Hmm. Sounds like a woman I once knew."

Emma nodded her head. "Aye. Bronwyn was a mule about gettin' married."

Christopher laughed. "You know I wasn't referring to my sister-in-law." He retrieved a hard peppermint treat from his pocket and popped it in Emma's mouth to stall her retort.

"Oh, really?" Emma inhaled and leaned back against him. "Who were ye talkin' about then?"

He placed a kiss upon the top of her head. "You, my pet." Lucky for him, Hereford had provided the right amount of motivation for her to marry.

"Me? It wasn't that I was determined to remain unwed."

"No?"

"No. I'd simply not met a man who tempted me to consider a union in which the man legally took over all me possessions."

"Ah. I understand. You didn't want to give up your

independence, yet here you are upon a ship, sailing away from it all."

"I believe in ye and yer plans."

Her humble words of faith in him filled holes in his heart he hadn't known existed until now. No one other than his deceased cousin Baldwin had ever expressed such total loyalty and faith in him.

She turned and captured his face in her chilled hands. "I love ye."

"And I love you."

THE HADFIELDS

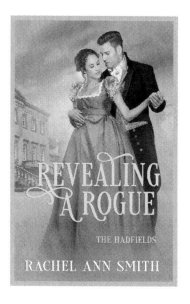

Book 1: Revealing a Rogue

For years she worked for him...

...and was loyal to a fault.

Why did she let herself yearn for a man, with whom she had
no future?

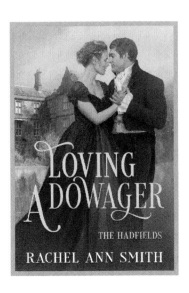

Book 3: Loving a Dowager

Will Henrietta Neale, the Dowager of Hadfield, reject the suit of a younger man or will she give love a second chance?

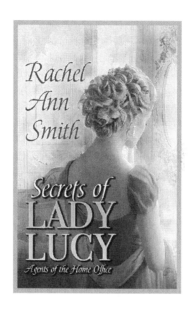

Book 1: Secrets of Lady Lucy

She is determined to foil an attempted kidnapping.

He is set on discovering her secrets.

When the ransom demand comes due—will it be for Lady Lucy's heart?

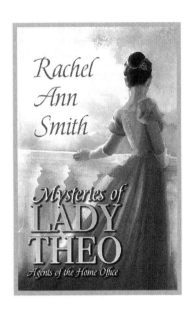

Book 2: Mysteries of Lady Theo

She inherited her family's duty to the Crown.

His duty to the Crown took priority.

Will the same duty that forced them together be what
ultimately drives them apart?

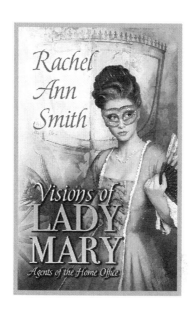

Book 3: Visions of Lady Mary

She wants a life of adventure.

He once called her a witch.

Will fate prevail or will Mary's stubbornness win out?

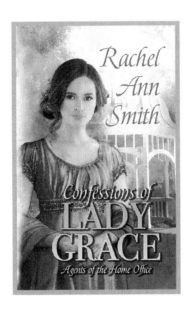

Book 4: Confessions of Lady Grace

She sacrificed her future to save his life.

He survived only to return home and find she is betrothed to another.

Will her confessions set them both free?

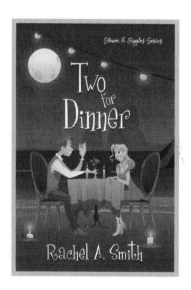

Damien

I'm done with work and women.

Except there is a bikini clad blonde standing her ground on *my* terrace.

Irene

What do you do after jilting a cheating fiancé at the altar?

Definitely not fall in love with a stranger who you nick name Mr. Merman.

Find out what happens when a reservation mix-up has these two stuck together on a remote island.

ABOUT THE AUTHOR

RACHEL ANN SMITH writes steamy historical romances with a twist. Her debut series, Agents of the Home Office, features female protagonists that defy convention.

When Rachel isn't writing she loves to read and spend time with the family. You will often find her with her Kindle, by the pool during the summer, or on the side-lines of the soccer field in the spring and fall or curled up on the couch during the winter months.

She currently lives in Colorado with her extremely understanding husband and their two very supportive children.

Signup for Rachel Ann Smith's newsletter for updates on new releases and monthly giveaways. www.rachelannsmith.com

Printed in Great Britain
by Amazon

65798385R00158